S&F

The Funeral Club

Richard D. Stafford

SF COMMUNICATIONS

TEXAS * GEORGIA

SF COMMUNICATIONS INC.
P.O. Box 8
Demorest, Georgia 30535

Copyright © 1993 & 1996 by SF Communications, Inc.

Cover artwork by Bill Stratton, Digital Impact Design, Inc., Cornelia, Georgia. Graphic Designer, Sara Zimmerman Huber.

Library of Congress Catalog Card Number TXU 555 223

ISBN 0-9650478-0-6

Stafford, Richard D., 1951

First Printing, March 1996

6 7 8 9 10 11 12 13 14

PRINTED AND MANUFACTURED IN THE UNITED STATES

U.S.A. $10.95
CAN $12.95

For
Small Towns

C H A P T E R   O N E

The women stood like courageous matadors, surrounding the body laden stretcher, as if to pay homage to a fallen hero who had been bloodied by the battle of life and death. Their grey hair, which typically bristled on the back of their wrinkled necks from laughter and surprise, now wilted in desperation and exhaustion. These were not adolescent warriors, they were well-experienced, insightful, and savvy women revered as queens of the community. On this day, surrounding their fallen comrade, they were quiet like geriatric angels floating in a Michelangelo fresco. The air coming and going from their lungs was steady, too steady, almost without pattern. The faucet which always dripped in clock-like rhythm creating a bright orange iron stain on the yellowing porcelain was dry. The equipment, the tools of their trade, which frequently gurgled and sucked lay without life on a near-by table. And the door – that damned old door – which normally echoed with thunderous bangs from all who attempted to heave it open, was now silent. The preparation room for over a century had never been so still, so quiet. Even though it was certainly a place where death lived, a place feared by most living souls, here, surprisingly, it was almost always a place of laughter and camaraderie. But not today, not now.

✿ ✿ ✿

Heddy rammed the heavy gurney into the weathered back door of Hunt & Larkin Funeral Home and in a tone of voice not often heard in similar businesses, let out an ear shattering cry.

"Open, damnit, you piece of crap!"

Even though the funeral home was a cornerstone of the community, the building was in need of serious repair. The prep room door, several inches thick and half a century old, hadn't opened properly in years. The determined woman, nearly sixty, had the grit of a Marine sergeant's mother. She growled again, shoved hard, and the body laden stretcher covered with a clean white sheet burst through the stubborn door as June, her helper, yanked hard from the inside. The door, aging and mulish, was no different than the five ladies that ran the place. In fact, the funeral home was a gathering place of earthy, well-seasoned spirits.

Heddy whizzed past her black assistant and

wheeled the gurney to the prep table. June stepped outside to pick up a man's brown scuffed loafer that had fallen off the stretcher during Heddy's ram rodding. At the table, the red-headed mortician whistled through a small gap in her front teeth for June to help but without hesitation transferred the remains to the slanted, white porcelain work space with a thud. June, a Jamaican by birth, just stood looking at the door with her jaw cocked to one side.

"We oughta get this door fixed," June sputtered.

"Why? It opened didn't it?" Heddy sing-songed.

June closed the ancient, paint-peeling door gently and turned around to help remove the white sheet. Too late. With a snap, Heddy pulled off the sheet like an auto salesman uncovering the newest model. A second brown shoe fell to the black tile floor with a thud as Heddy exclaimed, "Black Bag!"

"My favorite," the assistant replied in a deadpan voice. After fifteen years, June knew all too well that black bags normally contained the remains of individuals who had died a violent death.

The beautiful walnut-skinned Jamaican, her ebony hair pulled back in a French braid, positioned the gurney in the corner of the small room. She was careful not to nick her well-polished nails. She stretched thin rubber surgical gloves over her dark hands and placed clear goggles on her wrinkle-free face. Over her faded brown and black batik sarong, June put a rubber overcoat. This bright red coat and matching boots never displayed a noticeable spot of blood. June looked like a shiny red fireman from a page in a child's book.

June Glasscock came to the United States in 1976, immigrating through Miami. For several months she lived with her sister who had married a Jamaican American businessman, then moved to Atlanta during that city's boom years. Her job with Hunt & Larkin began when she read a help wanted ad in the *Constitution:*

"Mortician's helper needed in the foothills of the Blue Ridge Mountains, 90 minute drive from Atlanta. Good pay, pleasant working conditions, all benefits. Squeamish stomachs need not apply! Room provided. Winnsboro. Call Betty. 706/555-1010."

June caught a bus to Lanier County, where Winnsboro was located and was immediately offered the job. This was her fifteenth year to work at the white Victorian building that stood prominently on one corner of the town square. At one point or another almost all 10,600 residents of Winnsboro had been in Hunt & Larkin to bid farewell to a friend or relative.

Becoming a mortician's helper was a new experience for June, and even after fifteen years, there were still surprises in her job. She loved the four women with whom she worked and enjoyed the many unexpected events that occurred. Whenever confronted with an unusual case in the prep room, she shouted cheerfully, "Boo noo noo noos," a Jamaican expression for someone or something really special. After a while, Heddy, the chief mortician, picked up use of the expression. There they would be, looking over some three-hundred-pound blubbery naked, male corpse, chanting in unison, "Boo noo noo noos...boo noo noo noos!"

Each nearly sixty years old, June and Heddy were a matched pair who had relied on each other in good times and bad. Heddy was the ultimate risk-taker to whom nothing was sacred. Once, when her own car was in the shop, Heddy convinced June to accompany her to Grogan's Grocery in the hearse. There were only a few unwritten rules at Hunt & Larkin, but using the hearse for unofficial business was an absolute no-no, even here in this small southern town. Heddy didn't care, though. After working forty years for the Larkins, she felt secure.

The two rolled into Grogan's parking lot, pulled the long black coach up to the curb-side fire zone and jumped out. Several people who were leaving the only family food store in town watched to see if a body was going to be picked up. The presence of the hearse generated the same kind of interest as did the local fire truck when it was parked in front of the store. Once inside Grogan's, Heddy ordered June to push the grocery cart while she selected items from a rather extensive shopping list. Heddy shopped only once every two or three months and this was a two-cart venture.

At the meat counter Heddy exchanged obnoxious comments with Mr. Grogan about the similarities of their jobs. Grogan enjoyed the banter and tried to top Heddy's remarks. However, when other shoppers came within hearing distance, the two politely discontinued their bantering. This time, at the peak of some nasty comment, June ran down a nearby aisle to squelch her laughter and to pick up a bag of dried black beans.

After checking out the two senior ladies made their way to the hearse and helped a bag boy load the groceries through the extra wide rear door. Heddy placed the coffin stop, normally used to hold a casket in place, in an appropriate hole to keep the brown paper grocery bags from rolling around the back end of the Cadillac.

Curiously, Heddy asked the teenager if he had ever met her "Aunt Josey." The young man's eyebrows wrinkled down toward his nose and he replied politely, "No, ma'am."

"She's just coming out of your store."

The boy turned and looked back at the double automatic doors. Out came Joe Johnson, a fat, balding fifty-year-old slob in a dirty white undershirt, light blue shorts, and black shoes and socks. The boy broke up in laughter.

Heddy gave the young man a dollar tip and watched as he chuckled and walked back toward the whooshing doors. After just a few steps however, the kid turned around with the same inquisitive wrinkled look on his face and hollered back at the large red-headed mortician. "Hey, aren't you the lady that, uh, a couple of months ago, that uh..."

"Nope, not me!" Heddy was taken with surprise as if she had committed a crime and was just discovered.

"Yeah, you're her!" the sack boy observed with a quick laugh. "But you were drivin' a white Dodge."

"Not me, must have been another shopper. Bye!" Heddy jumped in the front seat of the hearse, smiled innocently at June and pressed the gas pedal of the long black coach to the floor.

Well, it was *indeed* Heddy. She had made her usual large shopping spree two months earlier and had taken her own groceries out to the car. She reached for the car door and found it locked. In fact, all the doors were locked. Heddy left the grocery cart next to the car and went inside to find someone to help her break into her car. The sack boy came out with a coat hanger and assured Heddy he could jimmy the lock. It took almost fifteen minutes, but the lad finally got the hanger in the right position to pop up the chrome lock on the driver's door of the old white Dodge.

"Thanks!" Heddy said, handing the boy a dollar for his efforts.

"Anytime," the youngster replied, loading the eight bags of groceries and supplies in the back seat. The kid locked the back door securely and deposited the bent hanger in a trash can by the front door of the store before going inside.

Heddy jumped into the front seat, swung the door shut, and slipped her red metallic Dodge key into the ignition on the steering column. She tried to turn the key and was surprised that it would not turn. The big lady wiggled the key several times impatiently, but to no avail. In one last, furious man-handle, Heddy crammed the key in again, almost bending the red metal shaft. Then her eyes dropped down to the cigarette tray. In it sat a plump, half-smoked moist cigar. Heddy's eyes widened as she noticed a yellow jacketed book on the passenger floorboard with the title, *Astrology: Now and Forever* printed across the cover. Heddy did not own an astrology book nor did she smoke cigars. In less than a milli-second Heddy Hedford jumped out of the Dodge, locked the door, and slammed it shut. She moved away as if it might bite her, hoping no one saw her — in that car — which looked amazingly like hers which was parked just two spaces away. Heddy walked toward *her* Dodge and then it hit her like a ton of bricks. Her groceries were in the back seat of someone else's automobile!

Heddy zipped back to the mistaken Dodge and lifted the back door handle, peering into her groceries. Yep, there they were, all safely tucked away in the back seat. She looked at the other three locks, all in the down position. The nearly seventy-year-old woman raised her head slowly above the car roof toward the store entrance wondering which customer owned the car. Her eyes shifted, scanning the entire front area of the parking lot.

"No one," she grunted. Heddy raced toward the automatic doors, nearly becoming her own funeral customer, as she played chicken with a passing delivery truck. Her red hair flying, Heddy zoomed through the door and quickly grabbed the same bag boy who was now sacking groceries for another customer. Heddy held the kid by his shoulders and steered him out through the rubber-matted entrance, snagging the bent coat hanger out of the trash can with one hand. All the way across the parking lot the teenager was hysterical waiting for an answer for Heddy's headiness. She deposited the boy at the car door of the mysterious Dodge.

"Open this door, now damnit!"

"But I just opened it for you a minute ago."

"Look, kid, I accidentally locked it after you left. My groceries are getting hot. Open it again and I'll give you another tip." Heddy kept looking toward the store doors anxiously hoping the owner of the Dodge would not emerge.

The wrinkles on the boy's forehead were now a mixture of inquisitiveness and fear, tainted with his suspicions about the woman's sanity. The boy kept a watchful eye on Heddy and struggled to open the door once again. More quickly than before, the knob popped up. Heddy shoved the high school student out of the way, unlocked the back door and grabbed bags of groceries. She handed them to the sack boy who stood absolutely astonished.

"Quick, hold these!" Heddy commanded like an army general, stuffing more and more bags of groceries into the boy's arms until his body disappeared behind brown paper sacks over-flowing with toilet paper, potato chips and other items from Grogan's Family Food Store.

Her own arms full, Heddy told the bag boy to follow her, which he did obediently and in great fear. The boy in tow, Heddy walked to her Dodge just two spaces away. Balancing bags of groceries, she opened the back door and began throwing bags in the back seat. She grabbed items from the kid and threw those in, too. Heddy reached into her jeans pocket and pulled out a five dollar bill, slammed it into the bag boy's sweaty hand, reached down to his head and gently closed his mouth which was wide open. Holding his chin shut, Heddy said,

"You won't remember a thang!" With that, Heddy slid into her car and sped away.

Two months later he did remember, apparently.

The two morticians unloaded Heddy's mass of groceries from the back of the hearse and took them inside the white, small frame house and then returned the big coach to its usual parking place behind Hunt & Larkin. The chief mortician took a soft cotton mitt and began shining the hood of the black hearse. June kicked the back door of the funeral home twice. It opened and she hurried upstairs to the apartment with her small bags of groceries.

Her cozy attic apartment was rent-free. It contained a large bedroom, sitting area and small kitchen where she would occasionally make Jamaican dishes to share with her comrades. The girls loved it when June cooked up a special island dish. One of June's favorites was Jamaican black bean soup with crab meat. An added advantage of the Caribbean cooking was that the odors canceled out the pungent formaldehyde smell that often drifted into the upper room. Cooking for the other women was a delight for June, but more importantly for her working at Hunt & Larkin gave her an opportunity to return home to Jamaica for a week each year. Going back to the island at Christmas meant everything to June. It was her perk, her holy place.

Heddy slipped into a freshly laundered lab jacket. Usually a clean jacket became disgustingly spotted with someone's "gift of life" within a short time. Just as Heddy's fingers touched the zipper of the black bag, the buzzer on the wall sounded and a gracious voice came over the nearby speaker.

"Heddy, would one of you gals come up front when you get a second, please."

Betty Larkin, sitting at her desk in the central parlor removed her finger from the black buzzer button and picked up the ringing phone.

"Hunt & Larkin, may I help you?" Betty answered in her customary, grandmotherly way. Hers was a caring voice that made all, whether confronted by a death or not, feel that everything was going to be okay.

"No, it's been changed. Mrs. Morgan will receive guests here tomorrow morning at eleven, and the funeral will be Thursday at two. You do know Mr. Morgan was...yes...that's fine, bye now." Betty idly rubbed her hand over the small mahogany box on her desk. Her gaze wandered to the street which was visible through the large Palladian window on the front side of Hunt & Larkin.

A few moments later June entered the central part of the old building, sans red rubber coat and boots. She carried a man's brown hat and a well worn green and brown striped tie spotted with droppings from several previous meals. The hat and tie seemed to be in remarkable shape considering how the man had died. Betty handed June a clipboard with funeral directions for the client in the prep room.

"I don't know how Heddy does it! And sometimes, I don't know how I even ended up here," June added with a chuckle as she adjusted her Jamaican wraparound. "It can really be eye opening even after fifteen years! Old Mr. Morgan was a Sunday School teacher at the Primitive Holiness Church, the congregation that handles snakes. But this is just too much. He's in there on the table, and did you know he..."

"If it's really bad, you could apply for the greeter's job at Mega-Mart?" Betty commented with a quick smile, and added, "They always hire people *our* age for that job, you know?"

Betty hushed June and politely reminded her that her monthly income allowed her the annual trek to Jamaica during the Christmas holidays.

June quietly placed the rumpled hat and tie on Betty's desk and settled into a big chair near by. The front door of Hunt & Larkin swung open and a casket spray of red roses floated in with Martha Rae Allison in tow.

"Hi y'all! Isn't this lovely?" she whispered loudly with her slightly out-of-place but friendly Texas accent.

"It's okay to speak up. No visitors." Betty whispered back, smiling.

"Good. I know it will be just beautiful on that wooden casket. Mary Beth Morgan picked it out. But ya know how I feel, so just tell me how it looks because I don't want to see the body," Martha Rae gushed, finally speaking in a normal voice.

Martha Rae wore a light blue sun dress revealing more than six decades of freckles on her shoulder tops. She wore a delicate gold necklace from which dangled a tiny "Texas" shaped pendant. Slightly over five feet tall, Martha was the shortest member of the Club. She looked up to everyone. She regularly used "Autumn Leaves" hair rinse which left her with a glorious auburn crown almost without a visible strand of gray hair. Her sunny personality was only occasionally darkened by a vocal and distinct fear of the slumbering "clients."

"Girls, why don't we just relax and forget about Mr. Morgan? I am sure Heddy has everything under control back there." Patting Martha Rae's arm reassuringly, she guided her to the couch and they both sat facing June.

"I realize working here can be exhausting and surprising at times, but you both knew what you were getting into when you took these jobs a long, long time ago, right? Now let's remain professional and show some dignity to our sleeping friends."

"I can be professional, I just don't care to find a..." June started to argue, but her voice trailed off. Martha got up and took the spray into one of the slumber rooms attached to the main receiving area and then entered the kitchen in search of morning coffee. The phone rang.

"Hunt & Larkin," Betty announced, "I'm sorry, it's been changed. The funeral is at 2 P.M. on Thursday at the Primitive Holiness Church. Yes, yes, you can...but I recommend you... Thanks, bye now."

Heddy looked through the small window in the prep room door. Seeing that no visitors were present, she strolled in *without* removing her lab jacket. Her customary faded jeans protruded below the coat. Her white coat was now slightly stained with Mr. Morgan's blood and she carried a long slender stainless steel tube with rubber hose.

"I can't believe they want an open casket," Heddy blurted, while shaking the silver tube. "That man was seventy-eight years old. What was he doing driving an eighteen-wheeler?"

"He wasn't driving an eighteen-wheeler. He was hit by one," Betty gently corrected, her back still turned to Heddy.

Martha Rae glided through the kitchen door. Seeing Heddy standing there in the blood spotted jacket, she dropped the tray, coffee cups, and spoons.

Betty sprang to her feet.

"Friends, let's remember this is a funeral home not a circus. Even though we are the only 'phone company' in town, we must maintain some semblance of professionalism...Heddy, do you mind removing your coat before you emerge? And please leave the trocar and all other instruments back in the preparation room."

Heddy turned toward the swinging door of the prep room and quipped, "You know there is more of Mr. Morgan on me than on that table back there. And figure this, not a scratch on his tattoo!"

Martha re-entered, with a towel from the kitchen, she bent down, picked up the broken cups, and mopped up the spilled coffee. As she scrubbed the rug, the loose skin below her chinless face wiggled left and right like turkey wattle. Martha, on the verge of tears, spoke haltingly.

"I am so sorry, Betty, but I just can't stand to see something like that. And the trouble is that Heddy just doesn't think anything about it. Might as well be some old dog they scraped off the highway."

Betty murmured reassurance as she blotted a coffee spot on the hem on her friend's sundress and helped gather the broken items. She sent Martha back for another coffee tray and retired to her desk.

June had remained in the chair watching the whole event. Her eyes were now fixed on some unseen object through the giant Palladian window.

"Boo noo noo noos," she whispered under her breath.

Rising, she shook her head and strolled back to the prep room, clipboard in hand. Once again, the phone rang.

"Hunt & Larkin. It's been changed. Oh, good, I am glad the word is getting around. Well, I don't think it should be open either but...yes, I know...Heddy will do the best with what... yes...okay, bye." Betty put back the receiver and turned as the front door opened. Louise Patton, the book keeper for Hunt & Larkin, stepped feistily inside. Her energetic entrance gave no hint of her seventy-one years.

Louise Patton, single by choice, sported a man's charcoal pin-stripe suit, white starched shirt, and a red and silver man's striped tie. Her shoes were glossy black and wing tipped. It appeared as if she were wearing men's black hosiery. For years it was rumored that if her pants legs were lifted, one might discover men's garters holding up the black nylon stockings. She was inseparable from her thin black brief case and proudly wore tortoise shell trifocals. A hint of cologne, something akin to English Leather, always traveled along with Louise. Her thick gray hair was shortly cropped and impeccably coiffed. Her fingernails were square at the tips and bore no polish. Louise, or "Lou" as she was known to intimates was often mistaken for someone's grandfather. The mistaken identity never bothered her. She just always laughed in a deep voice made husky by years of smoking.

"Morning. Here are the checks," she said in a raspy voice. Her manner was business-like as she flipped open the brass locks on her briefcase. Lou's upper and lower lips were drawn tightly together toward a center point as if she were sucking on an invisible straw. Her colorless mouth, free of any lipstick, more closely resembled an anus than a woman's lips. She acted as if she were handing over her personal money for the salaries rather than the income from Betty's funeral home. Watching every penny brought-in or paid-out by Hunt & Larkin had been Louise's job for almost fifty years. Cecil Larkin had hired her in 1942. He hired her soon after she graduated with a business degree from St. Agnes College, a private women's school in Atlanta.

Cecil bought the funeral home from the Hunt family shortly before World War II. The Hunts had originally opened a mortuary in Atlanta, but competition at the turn of the century had forced them out of business there. They had moved up to the North Georgian foothills, and established a funeral home where no others existed. The Hunts prospered. Cecil and Betty took over the business and carried on traditions that resulted in prestige for the company and profits for the owners. After years of commercial success, Cecil's widow, Betty, was wealthy enough to close the doors if she saw fit. But she didn't.

From the minute the guests stepped into Hunt & Larkin, the scent of carnations and roses was noticeable. The pleasant odor of flowers seemed present, even when there were no flowers in the viewing rooms. It was a permanent part of the structure, floating invisibly in the air from the countless thousands of funeral sprays honoring countless thousands of people now gone and perhaps forgotten.

The funeral home had been built as the Stephen's House in 1885, but was converted to a funeral home in 1901, when the wealthy family moved back North. The North Georgia humidity was just too much. The preparation room, at the back of the building, was actually where the kitchen was located when the structure was initially erected. From the floor to a height of five feet the walls were covered with white tile. Above the shiny tiles the plaster had been painted white, several times, and still needed a new coat of paint. The walls in the prep room, as in all of the rooms downstairs were eleven feet in height. On three of the white plaster walls hung white metal cabinets, containing all the apparatuses necessary to embalm bodies. The black tile floor was chipped.

A set of tall, wide, swinging doors joined the preparation room to what was formerly the dining room. The wall between the dining room and the living room had been removed in order to make the two areas into one large space known as the central parlor. The parlor was last wallpapered in 1970, in a soft brown and green fern print. After twenty years it was time to re-paper. The drapes were a rough beige material overlying sheer curtains. The beautiful oak floors were covered in areas with large Victorian rugs.

A long open hallway bordered the far side of the

parlor and ended at the front door. A twenty-foot runner made entering Hunt & Larkin a warm and welcoming experience. On the left side of the hallway were three doors which lead to the slumber or viewing rooms. These were formerly bedrooms, but now the staff referred to them by their colors.

The first slumber room, the "Green Room," had walls covered in dark, forest green silk wallpaper. Several tall wooden, plant stands were topped with green silk fern plants. The drapes were several shades of green striped material covering large Southern horizontal louvers painted a pale green. The woodwork in the room was painted the same light shade of green.

The middle room, the "Pink Room," was wallpapered and painted in every shade of pink imaginable. The rich pink drapes were lined with frilly white lace and anyone entering would suspect this room was most often used for viewing young children or ladies. On one wall there was a framed print picturing a Victorian love seat, draped on one end by a gentleman's coat. No individuals were seen in the print.

The third viewing room was the "Blue Room." This room was selected by many patrons. The large oval area rug contained a series of blue circles, in different shades, with a small white circle in the center. Deep blue velvet wallpaper was accented with several framed prints of ocean scenes. One picture featured a small boy with his back to the viewer. He was sitting on a sand dune, looking out upon the ocean.

On the front wall of the central parlor was the centerpiece of the room, a large Palladian window which contained panes of glass with a rippled, almost melting, antique look. Many sections contained tiny air bubbles, trapped miniscule pockets of virgin air from the 1890's. Viewed through one of the bubbles, the world outside had a strangely warped look. Across the street in what was formerly Jones' Hardware, was another giant window where the word CLOSED was written in oversized letters. It looked as though someone had written the letters on the inside of the large dirty window by erasing the filth with a rag, thus forming the giant word out of clean glass. Looking at it, through one of the larger ripples in the Palladian window, made the word appear to stretch completely across the downtown area.

Jones' Hardware was not the only vacant building in downtown Winnsboro. In fact, Hunt & Larkin was one of the last occupied businesses on the Square. Grogan's Grocery, owned by a family of the same name, had closed a year before. The Grogans had sold fresh meat, hand wrapped in white waxed butcher paper for seventy-eight years. Vida Jo Grogan retrieved the paper dispenser for use in her elementary classroom when the store closed. She often told stories of how her grandfather and father would tear off short pieces of paper with a quick snap, and wrap several pounds of fresh ground beef or a chicken.

Now, however, Vida's second-graders pulled off sections of newsprint from the black antique dispenser and drew pictures for their teacher, their moms and their dads.

Across the street from Grogans had been the M.F. Moses' Variety Store. It had closed three years ago. For generations kids bought school supplies at the Moses' Store and would spend their allowances there on Saturdays. The aisles were lined with flat counters containing glass dividers where all kinds of small surprises were displayed.

The variety store took its place in the business community when the bricked streets were new, shortly after the turn of the century. The well-worn bricks were still there but M.F. Moses was gone.

Next to Moses' was Copeland's Drug Store. In the nineteen seventies, Fred Copeland signed a contract with a national drug store supplier to sell its brands. Things looked uptown then; Fred's drug store even had a counter with spinning stools covered with red plastic Naugahyde. Years ago the old-fashioned soda equipment had been sold to a museum in Atlanta. More recently, customers could order a bottled soft drink, a cold chicken or tuna salad sandwich and a bag of chips. No cooked items though. A small sign taped to the mirror behind the counter read, "Parents, please do not allow your children to sit and spin on the stools." No one paid the sign any attention. Absolutely no one. Kids would spin around and around, some grown ups, too!

Fred couldn't stand the idea of selling his drug store to anyone; so, when he became ill last year, he just locked the door. His granddaughter did have hopes of becoming a pharmacist, but competition on the by-pass was too tough, and it just seemed inevitable to close the business. Now, the merchandise inside lay collecting dust instead of attracting customers. On the door a yellowing 3 x 5 card had been taped:

"Closed permanently. If you need prescriptions filled please see the Mega-Mart Pharmacist out on the by-pass. -- Fred"

That said it all. The by-pass. The Mega-Mart. The Wholesale Club. The new regional discount Super Food-Save Mart. These national, mega-buying giants housed under expansive metal roofs were catering to Winnsboro and Lanier County shoppers seven days a week, selling everything once sold downtown in smaller, separate stores. These new stores sold everything at discount prices. Several acres of black asphalt parking lots connected the stores, divided by even more new asphalt known as By-pass 323. For a half a mile, this five-year-old North Georgia "Las Vegas" strip had been luring a menagerie of customers through its doors. The parking lots rarely emptied.

One of the new stores even stayed open 24 hours a day.

In contrast, the large brick-lined parking lot *downtown*, almost always stood empty. It was surrounded by vacant buildings and beautiful maple trees. The only time it filled up was during funerals. When businesses had thrived downtown, funeral participants parked up and down the street under these giant maple trees. Now, with downtown deserted, it was easier for all simply to park on the Square. In a few days, local people would again park their cars on the Square and solemnly enter Hunt & Larkin to pay their last respects to a neighbor. These mourners would view one type of death inside, and another just outside Hunt & Larkin.

Winnsboro was once listed by US Retirement magazine as the second best community in the United States in which to retire. Taxes were low, as was crime, and the local citizens extended a true sense of hospitality to newcomers. Each evening, scores of people walked the sidewalks for exercise. The Winnsboro Mile, it was called. A unifying "sense of community" prevailed.

The area just outside the city limits, to the northeast, was part of the Chattahoochee National Forest. The Chattahoochee River, cool and crystal clear, had its start just a few miles to the northwest and ran right through Winnsboro and then continued south to Atlanta, where it became somewhat muddier and a lot wider. In the summer, folks came up from the city and floated on large, black rubber tubes down the pristine waters, allowing the bright summer rays to soak away their cares.

For years, the people in Winnsboro had resented the image drawn of them by the 1970's motion picture, "Deliverance." In fact, they were not a bunch of backwards hillbilly folks. In general, they seemed somewhat naive about the perplexing world of Atlanta to the south, but they maintained pride in their own civic affairs. The school still held a prominent role in town life and law and order were highly regarded words. T-ball, quilting and covered-dish church suppers occupied the time and energy of most residents. It was the kind of place where many people wished their grandparents might live. A place that would have made Norman Rockwell proud to paint.

The most distinguishable natural landmark near Winnsboro was Mount Yonah. From every highway entering the community, it could be seen rising 3,156 feet. Yonah, one of the tallest peeks in Georgia, had a distinctive "hump back" shape. In fact, the mountain appeared to look something like a giant sleeping bear, humped over for an eternal winter snooze. Residents who had been away from Winnsboro on trips always knew that home was close-by when they sighted the unusual three-thousand-foot slumbering bear. Yonah had always been there, signifying permanence, no matter what new business might come to town, or what old business might die.

The new mega retailers, out on the by-pass, with their extensive asphalt parking areas, created mixed feelings in the community. Many citizens enjoyed the convenience of having a wide selection of merchandise under one roof. There were others, though, who understood more clearly what loss of local downtown businesses did to the fabric of the community. It meant fewer Chamber of Commerce members and less support for civic and school activities. Ten years ago there were thirty-six ads in the high school yearbook, last year, ten. The new national quest for rural customers had gobbled up all but one business in downtown Winnsboro. Hunt & Larkin, stood alone and no one "outside" seemed to want it.

Heddy pushed a small metal bar on the automatic soap dispenser, located over the sink, and sanitized her hands in the pink, rose smelling goo which dripped to the stained sink. Suddenly, she burst back into the central parlor minus her white lab coat and the stainless steel aspirator, announcing,

"Just about through with old Morgan. As long as no one tries to peak at the snake, the decapitation will go unnoticed."

"Will you stop it? You have no dignity!" Betty chided.

"Well, the way I figure it, after about 3,000 embalms, they are all just the same to me. No emotion.

I could slab my own parents in the blink of an eye. Just a process."

Betty spoke, half sadly, "I hope you don't say that when I go."

"Sweetie, I'll go long before you do," Heddy laughed.

"And I'll go long before either of you," quipped Louise, the senior member of the Club, "Any visitors?"

"No, Mr. Morgan was in such bad shape I have discouraged everyone from coming by. Plus, with all the confusion over that wedding planned Thursday at the Primitive Holiness Church, just three hours before..." Betty purposefully avoided completing the sentence as she distractedly opened the morning mail which Louise had delivered.

"The Church members will be crying from sunup to sundown," June predicted. She entered from the prep room, replacing her pukka shell necklace around her neck as she walked.

Listening to all this, Louise, who normally did not allow herself levity added, "Hope people don't get confused and throw rice at Mr. Morgan. Might scratch the casket." All were shocked by Lou's attempt at humor. She drew a long sip of coffee as she enjoyed the response.

Not to be outdone by Louise, Heddy pensively added, "A wedding and a funeral...uhm...people will be coming and going all day...or uh, night." The ladies broke into laughter.

"Okay, okay, let's settle down," mother Betty pleaded, bringing discipline back to her flock.

"Are you ready for me to roll Mr. Morgan to the slumber room?" June asked Betty.

"Go for it," Heddy nodded approvingly, "and no peeking!"

Curious, Louise ventured, "What *are* we peeking at?"

"Morgan has a snake in the grass!" Heddy imparted. June giggled.

"I really feel sorry for him. If he ever knew that two old ladies were going to be cutting and poking around on him, naked on that table, I bet he would have thought twice before he got that tattoo," June explained.

"What tattoo?" Louise continued quizzically.

"Old Mr. Morgan has a python on his pecker!" Heddy revealed triumphantly. Heddy described in luxuriant detail how the long tail of the snake began uncoiling at Mr. Morgan's sternum and wound around his bowling ball stomach until it's head reached the tip of his uncircumcised penis. The women roared. June immediately began her chant, "Boo noo noo noos, boo noo noo noos!" All the ladies joined the Greek-like chorus.

Gradually the group regained composure. Martha Rae, whose eyes were still filled with tears and laughter, haltingly speculated, "You know, I wonder what it looked like when it was..."

"Functioning?" Heddy finished, adding that old man Morgan was uncircumcised.

"Yes. Just think of that thing slowly rising...looking more like a 'hooded cobra' than a python...in a darkened bedroom...with moonlight drifting through a window," Martha gasped.

"Boo noo noo noos, boo noo noo noos!" June shrieked.

The women again dissolved in laughter.

In a determined voice, Louise insisted, "Well, I have *got* to see this."

Heddy held out her large arm, preventing Louise from striding through the swinging doors and into the prep room.

"Sorry. This python is petered-out!" she said gleefully. "Actually, Morgan's not in good shape. The tractor-trailer decapitated him. He would fall apart before you could get his zipper down. You wouldn't want him to lose his head over a couple of old frumps gawking over his noodle? Besides, he was a *very* religious man!"

"Yes, a snake handler!" June added as a great silence hung over the ladies and their eyes widened in disbelief.

"Biblical, of course," June rectified. In unison, they gasped air and spewed one giant guffaw.

The phone rang. More than likely, another of Morgan's friends was wanting to know what day and time the funeral would be. Betty motioned silently with her arm toward the prep room and the women, still smiling and teary-eyed, hurried out so she could give another mourner the funeral information. Betty pulled an expensive pearl clip-on earring off her ear lobe and raised the receiver for the umpteenth time.

"Hunt & Larkin, may I help you?"

C H A P T E R   T W O

From the start, the voice on the other end of the line did not sound like someone merely desiring to learn more about Mr. Morgan's burial service. Betty could always tell *her* people. Often she knew the name of the caller without having to be told. This voice was different. It did not belong to someone from the North Georgia mountains. This individual was not a local mourner.

"Ms. Larkin, my name is Marcus Kline. I am a financial agent for Loemann & Loemann in Atlanta. I have been asked to contact you regarding your funeral home."

"Is there anything wrong?"

"Wrong? No, actually, I have been asked to visit with you about Hunt & Larkin."

"Visit?" Betty's curious but half annoyed tone was

now clearly audible.

"Yes. Loemann & Loemann is a real estate and commercial brokerage firm that purchases struggling businesses. We make improvements and then re-sell the real estate or business to other investors." Silence.

"Ms. Larkin, are you there?"

"Yes. I don't understand, why would I need you?"

"Well, honestly you may not need us, but we need you. We would like to purchase Hunt & Larkin. We are..."

"But my business is not struggling."

"I am sure it is not."

"Then why would you want to buy it?"

"Well, in all candor, we sometimes also buy smaller lucrative businesses and..."

"Mr., what was your name, Kline?"

"Yes?"

"You could not afford to buy this funeral home. Thank you. Good-bye."

"Ms. Larkin?"

Betty replaced the phone receiver in the cradle much harder than was customary. All others had now left the main room. They had gone to perform their respective duties: getting the flowers ready, touching up Mr. Morgan's face, and posting bills.

"How could this stranger be so casual and insulting?" Betty pondered. Her face grew red as she angrily contemplated the last phone call. The redness of her face contrasted sharply with her blonde, almost white, hair. Betty preferred a "Donna Reed" hair fashion. In fact, she first started wearing that style in the early sixties when that show was popular on television. She envied the main character, who had two beautiful children, a handsome husband, and an attractive, comfortable home.

For the first twenty years of their married life, Cecil and Betty lived in the apartment above the funeral home, where June now lived. They had to be there for late night jaunts to pick up "clients." Cecil was not romantic and he never seemed interested in children, so they never had any. Betty hadn't wanted it that way. She would have preferred several kids, even if having them grow up in a funeral home might have been awkward.

In 1966, Cecil and Betty moved into a large, new brick home that was paid for in full. Located on a side street between downtown and Winnsboro Springs Park, the new home had all the modern conveniences popular at that time; dishwasher, disposal, double oven, central vacuum system, and intercom in each room. One thing it didn't have was a nursery. Four bedrooms, no children.

For years, Betty dressed like and watched Donna Reed, assuming the character's caring, bright attitude about life. Thirty years later, she still maintained Donna's attitude and hair style. But Betty's blonde hair was little more than a memory. Cecil was a memory. Before dying he, with tremendous help and guidance from Louise, had made sure Betty would always be comfortable, even wealthy.

She shared her fortune with others liberally, though. Each spring she hosted the "Donkey-Basketball Game" in the Winnsboro High School gymnasium and always underwrote the five-hundred-dollar fee. As regularly as clockwork, on the last Saturday in April, each year, two men would show up in town. They had several trailers packed with black and brown donkeys, braying to be let loose on the hard boards, to entertain screaming Winnsboro High School supporters.

Each donkey was fitted with special black rubber booties that kept the varnished wood gym floor free from hoof scuffs. Other "encroachments" to the gym floor were handled by June. The Jamaican cleaned the floor after a donkey had an "accident." She would wear her bright red overcoat with matching boots and when a donkey excused itself, June would jump up off the bench, blow a silver whistle and head for the mess with a mop in one hand and a galvanized pail and shovel in the other. Sometimes she would start off with just a mop only, even though the donkey may have had a bowel movement. Then, the audience would scream, "Number two, number two!" June would scream back, "What?" Finally, June would retreat to obtain the correct cleaning tools and then swab the deck. The animals only seemed to tolerate

June, but her audience loved her.

During the game, five members of the high school basketball team would mount donkeys with red saddles and five people from the community would ride donkeys with blue saddles. Team members wore jerseys that matched their own color. The jerseys had obviously been worn by countless other people in different small communities.

Atop these stubborn animals, good sports of the community would play basketball. Few points were scored by either team, but the bedlam that ensued left the audience howling.

Heddy played for the community team. Her long legs allowed her black hightops to touch the wood floor as the animal galloped toward her team's goal. During the last donkey ball game, Heddy scored thirty-six points, making her the all time point scorer on either team since donkey basketball began in Winnsboro many years ago.

As the buzzer sounded and the community team won, June raced toward Heddy with a galvanized pail. The audience watched in disbelief as June hurled the bucket, spilling the contents over Heddy's head. To the surprise of all, it was only water, that June had placed in a different, and fortunately clean, bucket. The crowd cheered and laughed as they exited the odoriferous gym. Donkey basketball was a highlight each year in Winnsboro and Betty was responsible.

These days, Betty was a smart dresser. With no children or grandchildren for whom she could spend money, she felt perfectly free to wear stylish clothes.

She always gave the other ladies birthday presents and bonuses at Christmas. In addition, to each of them she gave an annual cash present when they went on vacation. June's arrival fifteen years ago prompted that practice. June wanted to visit relatives in Jamaica so badly that Betty helped make it possible. Having helped June, she decided to give all of the women extra money for a vacation. The vacation destinations of the individual women were quite divergent.

Heddy always went to Orlando and spent several days "in the sun" as she told it. However, everyone knew she actually played in the theme parks. She was spotted by Vida Jo and her children who were on holiday at Disney World.

Louise, as expected, would simply deposit the gift into her checking account. She, like Betty, had no children. Everyone in town wondered who would inherit her countless hundreds of thousands of dollars. No one knew.

Martha Rae always used her summer bonus to travel to Texas to be with her brothers. Both of them were ranchers and avid hunters. Going to Texas was important to her because she had lost a son there. He was buried in the family cemetery on her brothers' ranch. So it was off to the Texas hill country near San

Antonio, for Martha Rae each year.

Martha Rae was born to wear slacks. When it became acceptable for Southern women to wear slacks and suits in schools and business places in the sixties, Martha Rae was ecstatic. Her favorite color was blue because it was so royal, just like her personality. If you looked in Martha Rae's closet you would find blues in every hue and pattern. There were slacks and pants in dozens of shades of blue. She was a soft blue flower in human persona.

Martha Rae joined Hunt & Larkin the same year as June. Before that, she had worked for Batson Flowers and often made floral deliveries to Hunt & Larkin. Betty realized Martha would be a positive asset to the funeral home after she observed her consoling the parents of Stephen Davis.

Stephen was one of those young people most adults wished was their own child. His name regularly appeared on the honor roll of Winnsboro High School. The youth attended the Methodist Church and was usually the center of any group of local young people. He had a special fondness for Betty Larkin and helped her by mowing the rich green grass around the stately white building each summer. More recently, he was saving his earnings to purchase some scuba equipment.

His head was covered with thick dark hair which, if allowed to grow, would become small curls. His complexion looked perpetually tanned, although no one seemed to know how it got that way. His parents, employees of a local bank, were much lighter in skin tone and hair. The source of his genes was a true mystery and he was, reportedly, often teased as a young boy for having been adopted.

Stephen enjoyed competitive swimming. Being in the water was everything to the sixteen-year-old boy. He had swum on a team in Atlanta for five years before moving with his parents to Winnsboro. He was such a popular fellow, that friends and townspeople would often drive back to Atlanta to watch him compete since Winnsboro did not have a swim team. Stephen had a big following at the meets. He wore a black Speedo swim suit that showed off his sleek, muscular body. The only apparent blemish on this young Adonis was a brown mole on the inside of one ankle, shaped like a kidney.

The first summer Stephen moved to Winnsboro, he spent a lot of time at the city swimming pool. He was eleven years old and had already won many ribbons in Atlanta. Early one August morning in 1971, Stephen was swimming laps at the pool. The city employee responsible for cleaning the pool had brought his four year old son to work. While the father was distracted in the pump house, the toddler fell into the pool. Stephen, resting nearby from his laps, dove after and rescued the youngster. Had he not been there, the child probably would have drowned. The Davis boy was a hero from the start.

In July of 1976, during the bicentennial celebration weekend, Stephen disappeared. No one could imagine where the sixteen-year-old had gone. His disappearance was unusual because his relationship with his parents was completely normal. He wasn't at all the kind of youngster who would run away. Less than a day later, a massive hunt began.

People from as far south as Atlanta began to search for Stephen. His sophomore school photo that showed his thoughtful brown eyes and just a hint of adolescent mustache, was broadcast on every Atlanta television newscast.

The evening of July 5th, his body was located. A resident on Lake Burton, only a few miles from Winnsboro, found the boy's body near his dock at the water's edge. Stephen was wearing his characteristic black Speedo and appeared to have drowned. Laboratory blood analysis revealed a small amount of alcohol in his blood stream and that death was, indeed, by drowning.

The ensuing investigation turned up the name of another local high school boy, Jimmy Johnston, who had told a friend that he and Stephen had been at the lake together the evening of July the 4th. The Johnston boy had little in common with Stephen and had seemed somewhat jealous, at times, of the younger, better looking student. Johnston had only one thing Stephen wanted, a car.

An investigation, which never resulted in an

arrest, was ruled an accident. The report revealed a strange story of either tremendous jealousy and intimidation or incredible misfortune. The two youths had gone to Lake Burton in Jimmy's car. They'd planned to swim at dusk and to watch the fireworks afterwards. Stephen who envied Jimmy because he had a car, was most willing to befriend the older teenager.

Burton, a long narrow lake, of absolutely clear water, was surrounded by steep banks that were thickly covered in pines and poplars. Most homes had been on the lake for decades, and had been occupied by successive generations of the same families. Vacant lots had not been available for many years. It was an old established lake, surrounded by families who knew the shorelines well and were not always ready to share the beauty with outside developers.

The boys had drunk a few beers. It was, in fact, the first time that Stephen Davis had ever had anything alcoholic to drink. While he was able to maintain the image of adult perfection among his peers and family, this night apparently he became a victim of an adolescent prank. A prank that, under more normal circumstances, would have become something to laugh about years in the future.

The boys lay on a long wood dock and finished the last of a six pack of beer. Jimmy held a powerful search light in his hands and lazily moved it back and forth. It shone like a laser beam on a few low dark clouds overhead. Earlier, the clouds had glistened with red, blue and green bursts of color from the fireworks around the lake. The clouds had become a fine mist. The night was moonless and pitch black. The two boys took turns spotlighting docks on the other side of the lake, a distance of about three-quarters of a mile.

"Jesus, look at that ski boat hanging in the boat sling over there," Jimmy observed, focusing the beam of light on a dock house some distance away.

"Yeah, it belongs to the bank president. I've been on it several times. It's fast and smooth." Stephen spewed the last sip of his third beer into the lake. "How do people drink this crap?"

"You get used to it. Think they can see the light beam?"

"No, don't think so. My mom said they invited several bank families for fireworks at Piedmont Park in Atlanta but my folks have to spend every day with the guy so they decided to stay here. You can see everything with the light. Wonder what it looks like from over there?"

"Don't know," the Johnston boy quipped and then flicked the beam of light off-and-on several times and continued, "Hey, why don't you swim the lake?"

"Swim the lake?"

"Yeah, you stay here, and I'll go to the other side and guide you with the light. Kinda like radar."

"Jimmy, that's a long way, even for me."

"It's less than a mile, probably like half a mile.

How many laps can you swim non-stop in the pool?"

"I can swim a mile easily, but..."

"But what? What are you afraid of? I'll guide you like one of those scud missiles. Just follow the light. It's simple."

"Man, I don't know." Stephen sat there, his black swim suit still damp, from an earlier swim, under his snug fitting jeans. "I'm a little dizzy. It's been a long time since we ate slaw dogs, and this beer..."

"Wussy, you couldn't do it anyway."

"Wait, what ya mean I couldn't do it?"

"You have on a wussy swim suit and you are a wussy. It's that simple." A prankish smile lit his white face which was almost invisible in the dark.

"Look, why would I..." Stephen sat up and glanced across the lake. It was black. Most of the lake houses were dark.

"Naw, it's a stupid idea..." recanted Jimmy.

"No, I'll...I'll do it. I'll do it."

With that Stephen pulled off his bright red University of Georgia tee shirt, removed his leather deck shoes and peeled off the damp jeans. He folded the clothes neatly and placed them on his shoes.

"Take my stuff with you, across the lake. Their name, 'McKinney' is on the mailbox by the driveway. It's a wood house painted yellow. You can't miss it. Flash the light three times when you get to the dock, by the speed boat. I'll start then." Stephen directed with a controlled adult voice.

"All right!" The older boy laughed out loud.

Jimmy made his way back to his 1976 Camaro, which was parked just beyond the fishing dock. The light bobbed up and down as he walked. It rested atop the pile of Stephen's clothes that Jimmy carried like laundry in his arms.

The car started and pulled away as Stephen sat on the end of the dock contemplating the goal. Swimming was natural for him. It had been natural back when he first swam in Atlanta at age five. Natural when he competed in youth swim meets, and won many blue, first-place ribbons. It was natural for him when he saved the boy from drowning at Winnsboro Springs Park the first month he and his parents moved to the community. There was no problem here. Less than a mile was the distance to be covered. He had exceeded this distance in a pool many times. Yes, he was a little lightheaded from the beer, but he was certainly not drunk.

He could hear, but not see, the water gently sloshing on the wooden piers. He sat on the edge of the dock, his feet gently skimming the black surface below. He waited patiently for Jimmy to flash the light from across the lake.

Twenty minutes passed. Then three flashes came. The light was brilliant. Like a solid white beam, a stick, reaching out to guide him safely to the far side of Lake Burton. The young man stood and placed his feet together, hearing in his mind the phrase he knew so well, "SWIMMERS TAKE YOUR MARK!"

His long legs were crouched in their customary position, and his arms were stretched out to a point. As if he heard the sharp crack of a starting pistol, Stephen Davis leaped quietly, like an otter, into the dark waters of Lake Burton.

In seconds he came to the surface and focused on the shaft of brilliant light. Gliding along the surface, the light seemed even brighter, its reflection mirrored on the shimmering surface. Stephen did not struggle as he swam. He imagined himself to be a giant commercial aircraft, landing safely in the fog as landing strip lights broke the darkness. With every stroke the light became brighter. Like a slivering seal the young boy did the butterfly, the back stroke and finally the freestyle, changing regularly so as to rotate the use of all his muscles.

He was less than halfway across the lake when the light went dark. Stephen took a few more strokes and then stopped for a moment, continuing to kick his legs under water to stay afloat. He yelled. "Jimmy! Turn on the light! It's not funny. Turn on the light!" the adolescent voice broke.

"Shit," he whispered, one arm reaching out in front, grabbing for water, searching for light. After a few moments, the light came back on, and Stephen once again focused on the beam. His legs were beginning to tire but he dared not stop his rhythmic pace towards the light.

"What the hell does he think he's doing?" Stephen thought, switching to the butterfly. "Maybe he's not doing anything. Maybe the light is burning out, a short, dead batteries or something."

Stephen continued and again the light went off and on for several seconds. He was about half way now but could make out nothing in the darkness. This time the light seemed to stay off for a longer period of time. Endlessly it seemed. Stephen tried to concentrate on the direction he had been swimming, but he wasn't sure. He continued and then stopped.

He looked back to where he had started. He could barely see a dim street light through the thick poplar trees behind the dock. He thought about turning around. After all, he had been swimming for almost twenty minutes. He could aim for the street light, swim twenty minutes and be back, safe at the dock. No, he was halfway now. The light would come back on. He'd be able to reach the McKinneys' speedboat.

Again the light went off. It stayed off. Stephen tried to focus on where the light had been, but it was impossible. He swam some more and then began to panic, something he had never done before in all his years in the water. He felt isolated, alone. He called out for Jimmy over and over again, but there was no answer.

Small goose bumps appeared on the lad's torso and arms. The fine dark hair on the back of his neck bristled. His breathing increased, as did his heart rate.

He was in trouble. The very thing that had brought him so much joy in life was now placing his own existence in great peril.

Confused, Stephen decided to turn back. Now he could not see the street light. "Where was it?" A small boat was passing in the distance, near where he first dove into the water and he focused on the red and green light mounted on the bow. The boat was moving slowly, perhaps trolling, looking for a catch. Stephen swam toward the boat, yelling for help, but the small craft was too far in the distance. No one heard him.

He stopped for a moment wanting to raise his body up out of the lake like Jesus and walk to safety. After all, he had always been the kind of kid who did what was right. Surely a miracle was in order here. He tried pushing his body out of the slippery water with his fists. Pushing and shoving hard, downward, with great thrusts only tired the youngster more. He began to cry. His energy was sapped. Stephen once again tried to swim toward where the light had shown. No luck, there was only darkness. He yelled for help. He cried aloud, wanting nothing more in the world than to touch something, anything on the bottom of his feet, to grab something, a buoy, with his arms. Nothing.

Finally, an incredible light of even greater intensity than the original beam shown in the distance. Stephen was calmer and swam toward the warm beacon with great confidence, as if to win the latest swim meet. In seconds, the sleek sixteen-year-old slipped beneath the surface of Lake Burton, a victim of the very thing for which he cared so much.

Mr. McKinney heard about Stephen's disappearance. The next afternoon, he went out to the dock, and made the gruesome discovery. The boy's body was lying in just a few feet of water beside the dock, distorted by the gentle lapping of waves. A large chrome flashlight sat on the other end of the pier, the switch in the "off" position.

Stephen's parents were devastated. They quit their positions at the bank and moved, almost immediately back to Atlanta. It was learned later, they had divorced but no one had heard from them after that. Stephen was their only son.

During the mourning period, Betty observed Martha Rae helping to console those arriving at the funeral home. There were hundreds, of visitors during the week, many from Atlanta. The Davises lived at the funeral home for three days, not even sleeping those nights at home.

Martha Rae never left the couple's side, trying to help both understand their loss. Martha's own son had died in an hunting accident in Texas at age thirteen. She knew firsthand the pain experienced by the parents. The only thing allowing Stephen's father and mother to make it through the three days was Martha's ability to relate her own loss.

Preparing Stephen's body was not business as usual for Heddy and June. Sometimes they made jokes about those they were working on, particularly strangers. This case was different. The two adored the teenager who kept the front lawn manicured in the summer. Though lifeless, the boy retained his good looks. He was the frozen likeness of a Greek youth. His tanned face appeared only to have fallen asleep. The Jamaican woman gently washed and caressed the youth's smooth forehead. She shampooed his black curls, wiping small quiet tears from her equally black cheeks. The death of this handsome youngster seemed so tragic.

They dressed the boy in a navy blue sweater, white button-down oxford shirt, and red tie, then slipped him into a silver metallic coffin, which Martha Rae had chosen. The Davises proved emotionally unable to make that decision. Normally, visitors were not present when a body was moved from the preparation room to a slumber room. Since Stephen's parents refused to leave, the casket was wheeled to the Blue Room in their presence.

When the mother and father first saw the coffin moving through the main parlor, they held each other in shock and sank to the floor. As they wept, Martha Rae, seeing an image of her own thirteen-year-old son in her mind, eased down beside them. They knelt there together, sobbing. Soon, they approached the slumber room and sat on the couch facing the open casket. They sat there crying softly seeing only the soft black hair of Stephen above the edge of the casket. On the wall behind them was the watercolor painting. The young boy sitting on a sand dune covered with sea oats, back to the viewer, looking out to sea.

This was no ordinary funeral home, no ordinary funeral staff. No matter how tragic a death seemed, this group of women helped those suffering feel more capable of facing the future without their loved one. Nothing could ever remove the pain, that was understood. But in the midst of grief, this place, Hunt & Larkin, and this kind person, Martha Rae Allison, had made it bearable, at least for a time. It would be difficult to find any place, anyone who could have done it any better.

C H A P T E R   T H R E E

The thoughtful care Betty and her girls gave people in the community and that Betty, herself, showed her associates made Hunt & Larkin a unique place of business.   Betty provided the mortar that held these human bricks together. Corporate America could have learned a thing or two by closely examining her style of leadership at the funeral home. Employees at the Mega-Mart probably could never feel the same about *their* founder, as Heddy, Louise, June and Martha Rae felt about Betty.

The day before Mr. Morgan's funeral, the women went right to work completing their various assigned duties. After Heddy prepared Mr. Morgan, she went out to Winnsboro Cemetery and helped Mrs. Morgan and her grown children select the right plot for their husband and father. After the relatives left, Heddy discussed the site with ol' man Jackson. Using a trenching tractor, he dug the plot four feet wide, eight feet long, and four and one-half feet deep. Jackson, who was also beyond sixty years of age, set up a dark green canvas funeral tent, and carefully lined three rows of ten chairs on the well-worn Astro Turf.

At the funeral home, Martha made sure the rose spray was properly placed on Mr. Morgan's casket and carefully arranged all the other flowers in the Green Room, all the while studiously avoiding peering into the casket.

On the day of his funeral, Martha went to the Morgan's home and set a large silver-plated coffee urn on the dining room table and positioned several dozen glass coffee cups alongside creamer, sugar and artificial pink and blue sweeteners. Before leaving, she placed a pretty fresh flower arrangement on the table and left open a guest book for friends and family to sign. Outside, several hundred feet down the street in both directions, Martha Rae placed yellow "PLEASE DRIVE SLOW-FUNERAL GUESTS" signs in the parkways.

As usual, about twenty minutes before the two o'clock service, Heddy and June collected the various flower covered crosses and upright sprays from the funeral home and delivered them to the Holiness Church, located several blocks from the Square. Once the guests had been seated, Martha and Betty escorted the family members to the church and into the first three rows of seats. Heddy and June swiftly followed behind, loading the casket in the hearse, driving down the street to the church, and then gently removed the casket, placing it on the church truck. The truck was a chrome-plated dolly with large wheels. It's gray rubber wheels crackled on the rice left behind by the wedding celebrated earlier in the day. Heddy and June positioned the casket in the narthex as Betty gracefully walked to the chancel area of the church and asked the congregation to rise.

Joseph Miller played "Nearer My God To Thee" on the Hammond, as every strand of his soft white hair sat in perfect place. His white bushy eyebrows were a canopy for the thin, red splotchy skin that sagged somewhat on his face. Joseph, also in his twilight years, played the organ with a fancy flare typical of a small, country church organist. He rocked to the left and right with a slight upward movement at his farthest right position, as if he were riding gentle waves in a tiny boat. His long, nimble fingers never missed a single note, even when his eyes were closed, which they were most of the time. The organ was, simply enough, an extension of the man who played it.

The casket was rolled into the sanctuary and positioned with the head end on the left, and the feet on the right. Heddy and Martha did the honors, making sure they had the casket correctly set.

Several years ago, during a Catholic service held at the Presbyterian Church (because Winnsboro didn't have a Catholic Church) Heddy accidentally placed the head of the casket to the right, meaning the coffin would have had to open on the side away from the congregation, with the lid blocking the view. For the deceased, it would have provided a wonderful view of the alter and pastor. Fortunately, just seconds before the service was to begin and after glancing at Betty's eyes, which were rolling around in their sockets while her head made a rotating movement, Heddy realized the mistake and rotated the casket once, repositioning it correctly. After the service, one of the Catholic family members gently clutched Betty's arm and sincerely whispered,

"How thoughtful it was of your associates to make the "sign of the cross" with father's coffin. Our family appreciates your caring and acknowledgement of our faith."

Betty just smiled in agreement, containing her delight until later when she shared the observation with Heddy and the others.

Once in place, Mr. Morgan's casket was opened, as requested. It is unusual to open a casket when someone dies from such a violent death as being run over by an eighteen wheeler truck. Sometimes, when family members request an open casket following a violent death they hope to intensify anger for whomever is responsible for the death. Betty would always discourage such a decision, but she had to yield when ever a family requested. In this case, Mr. Morgan's head lacerations were hidden under his hat and only a small amount of white gauze was visible near the back of his head. His secret tattoo was forever hidden beneath his starched white shirt and gray slacks.

Once the casket was opened and the service begun, Heddy retreated several rows back and sat quietly with June. Both gals wore navy blue business-like suits which were kept on a pair of wooden hangers in the prep room. They would jump into the dress suits just before loading a casket for a funeral. Settled, Heddy watched Morgan's nine year old grand nephew who was just in front of her. He had a red rubber band secured between his pointing finger and his thumb, simulating a rubber band gun. The lad kept "cocking" his thumb, and pointing the longest finger in all directions. His mother, focused on the service, ignored his every action. About half way through the service, during a prayer by Reverend Griggs, the wide rubber band zinged off the boy's finger, flew through the sweet air, and crash landed on Mr. Morgan's bulbous nose, surprising only Heddy and the boy who had their eyes now firmly fixed on the deceased. The rubber band lay there, perched on the vein-covered proboscis for the rest of the service and probably would have stayed there for all eternity had Heddy not snagged it when she closed the lid. Otherwise, some future generation might have discovered the rubber band in an archaeological dig and presumed it to be a relic of some cultural ritual.

Following the funeral service, the casket was reloaded in the hearse and transported to the cemetery with friends, relatives, and a nine year old with a very nervous finger in tow. It was a beautiful day with blues skies, and this made the event tolerable for all. When it rained during a funeral, the graveside service was always a difficult event for the women to conduct. They were lucky this day. Heddy guided the six pallbearers as they removed the casket from the black Cadillac and gingerly placed it on the lowering device between the chrome tower heads.

Mrs. Morgan had selected a weather tight steel vault that would keep out every drop of water and conceivable pest, thus preserving the old man and his snake tattoo for hundreds of years. After the mourners left, Heddy and June used a crank to lower the casket into the vault and carefully positioned the vault lid, securing the cover with several flip locks. The flowers were moved away, and ol' man Jackson drove up on his small front-end loader to replace the moist, red Georgia dirt. Once finished, he flashed Heddy and June a smile through missing teeth and drove the green tractor back to the garden house.

Heddy and June replaced the flowers and headed back to Hunt & Larkin in the Cadillac, leaving the site groomed for another visit by a few family members the next day. Thus the funeral home staff members ended their three-day commitment of quality and personal service to community members.

In late October, several weeks after the phone call from Mr. Kline, a certified letter arrived at the Winnsboro Post Office. The return address read, "Loemann & Loemann." At first, Louise, who had picked up the mail that morning thought about opening the envelope which was addressed to Betty Larkin. But she didn't.

As Louise strode through the front door, a small burst of wind blew half a dozen bright orange and red maple leaves, like tiny magic carpets, into the parlor. Outside, a dozen giant maple trees lined the parkway like soldiers between the sidewalk and street. Cecil had planted the trees years before, to provide summer shade for people gathering to visit their recently-departed loved ones. The trees were one asset the business-row out on the loop did not have.

Every October the twelve trees transfigured the street into a festive Indian summer parade of orange, yellow, and red. For a few weeks, this small part of Georgia resembled a miniature Vermont. Some people said the color was caused by the cool air blowing down from the Blue Ridge and others argued it was the large amount of rain water and humidity. Whatever the cause, the turning leaves were a breathtaking sight that lasted only a few days and then were gone.

Louise picked up the leaves and arranged them in a pen holder atop Betty's desk. Alongside them, she placed the daily mail, including the certified letter from Loemann & Loemann. Betty emerged from the kitchen with a cup of coffee as Louise took a seat in the large leather chair next to the desk.

"Jamaican coffee?"

"Trying to quit," Louise explained curtly as she placed her briefcase flat on her lap.

"Oh, look at the leaves. They're wonderful," Betty responded while clutching her white coffee cup sporting a yellow smiley face.

"The wind from the east floated them magically into Hunt & Larkin and they fell softly into your makeshift vase."

This little affectionate flourish was uncharacteristic of Betty's stern bookkeeper.

"Louise, how, uh, poetic sounding," complimented Betty, surprised enough.

"Thought you might need a boost before you open that letter."

Betty glanced down to see the letter with two thin, green remnants of a certified mail card taped to the envelope. She picked it up, squinting as she made out the words, Loemann & Loemann.

"What is it?" Betty reached for her letter opener.

"Isn't that the name of the company Mr. Kline represents? Remember, Mr Kline with the offer to buy us out?" Louise reminded Betty.

"Yes. It is."

Betty opened the letter and pulled out its single page.

"Dear Mrs. Larkin:

I would like to apologize for obviously disturbing you several weeks ago on the phone. The fact is, I never intended to do that. I know you are very attached to your business and I do not want to upset you. Please allow me to review your present situation:

1.) Your building is old and needs replacing,

2.) You are past a normal retirement age.

3.) Families expect modern services, like crematoria, these days.

4.) The downtown area in Winnsboro is not currently the best atmosphere for a business like yours.

Mrs. Larkin, I, too, am near retirement age. I understand how you feel. If there is any way you would consider selling Hunt & Larkin, my associates and I would like to make the purchase. Our investor, a large funeral home chain out of Macon, has given me approval to offer you $250,000 for your business. Please, seriously consider this offer. If you fail to accept it, our investors may elect to open a *new* funeral home in Winnsboro. The competition will not be good for Hunt & Larkin. Please let me know as soon as possible if you are interested in discussing the offer.

Sincerely,

Marcus Kline for Loemann & Loemann Investors"

Betty dropped the letter on her desk and leaned her head against her hand. She tapped her temple with two extended fingers, speaking more to herself than to Louise.

"What do you think they are trying to do?"

"Buy us out."

"Yes, I know, but there has been a locally-owned funeral home on this spot for almost one hundred years. They can't just march in here, throw some money in out face, and tell us to get out." Betty was now tapping the whole side of her face with the palm of her hand.

"Betty, they do have a point. Kline is right. The building is outdated. It is in need of some major repairs, if not complete renovation. Heddy can't get the clients in the back door. We are a couple of old ladies who should be drinking Bloody Marys at a condo on the South Florida coast. Our own years are dwindling just like the life of downtown. Even the leaves are dropping dead." Louise reflected while cleaning her glasses and pointing at the pencil holder.

"When was the last time a Winnsboro family asked for a cremation?" Betty asked indignantly.

"Never."

"Case closed."

Louise reached in front of Betty, seized the letter, and placed it back into the envelope. She popped the locks on her briefcase and slid the envelope inside, next to a pack of cigarettes. Her mouth made that funny straw-sucking movement. She brushed at the white hair grown down over half her ears, a sign it was time to have it cut. Louise closed and locked the briefcase over Mr. Kline's letter.

"OK." Louise looked at her stainless steel man's watch, stood and headed for the door. Her exit allowed yet another sharp breeze to scatter the leaves off Betty's desk and momentarily whisked away the carnation odor of Hunt & Larkin. Betty replaced all but one of the colorful fall leaves in the pen holder. She held up the last leaf and looked intently at its color, made brighter by the light coming through the giant window. The tiny veins appeared to carry nutrients, still, to its parts. It did not look dead to her.

Louise walked briskly down the street toward home, a two-story house not unlike the funeral home. On arrival, she hurried inside. Louise seldom turned on more than one light at a time. She used only two rooms of the five bedroom home. One room was set up as an office, and another as her bedroom. Louise went directly to her office.

Years before, the first week Louise worked for Cecil, an interesting event occurred. Cecil had just bought the funeral home from the Hunt family. It was mid-December. He had owned the business for almost a month and not one person had yet died. A call finally came that a man lay dead on the Square. It was four o'clock on a Sunday morning when a sheriff's deputy called. The thermometer had not risen above 25 degrees that evening. Cecil slipped on his pants and shirt, a heavy coat and walked outside to survey a grim scene. Across the Square, in front of Grogan's Grocery, a deputy was squatting beside a dark heap. He rushed over to find his first "client."

Muzaun Briggs, a local man known as "the night watchman," was frozen stiff in a fetal position. For years, Briggs, a half-wit, had walked around the Square at night keeping guard over local businesses while the town slumbered. No one knew exactly when the guy began his self-appointed patrol. Several times, through the years, the watchman had alerted authorities in the deep of night of emergencies; a small fire in the back of Grogran's, and several auto accidents on the Square. He was a town fixture from way back.

Apparently the old fellow had had a heart attack or fallen asleep in the cold, a victim of apnea. An autopsy was not conducted as it was assumed the death was innocent and most likely caused by exposure. At any rate he was frozen stiff, or as the deputy put it, "He's a froze *stiff*."

Cecil went back to the funeral home and drove the shiny black hearse to the scene. The coroner had arrived and pronounced the "town watchman" dead. The three men loaded the icy body onto a stretcher and then inside the hearse. The black Cadillac pulled up to the prep room door of Hunt & Larkin, and the three unloaded the client. It took all day -- using an oscillating fan -- to thaw the corpse and stretch the legs out flat. Finally, the body was prepared. Cecil was not able to find any next of kin and the county had no provisions to pay for pauper burials. It was all up to Cecil.

He talked over the need for a casket and burial plot with Louise. The young college graduate, eager to balance the budget, suggested finding some other way to pay the burial expense, but Cecil insisted that the funeral home bear the costs. Louise reminded Cecil that he had had no patronage during the first few weeks of operation. Cecil stood firm and Mr. Briggs was given a $150 casket and a $50 cemetery plot. Louise nearly choked with frustration when Cecil decided on a grave marker pronouncing "The Night Watchman, Muzaun Briggs." The day after Briggs was buried, Louise ordered the granite marker, as instructed, and even at this early age of twenty-two, her mouth pursed slightly. She did not often see things from Cecil's standpoint.

Even after fifty years, Louise still watched every dollar with hawk eyes. She was always looking for the best deal for the Larkins, even if they didn't want it. It was not that she didn't care about others; she just took her financial responsibilities very seriously. Except once, while on a recent trip with her comrades.

June, half jokingly, invited her four friends to Jamaica during one of her annual Christmas trips back home. Surprisingly, they all accepted the offer. It would, of course, mean the ladies would have to miss the annual performance of The Nutcracker, performed by the the Hoppin' Stompers. The Stompers were a group of young girls who clogged. Clogging, a style of country tap dancing in unison, was most popular in Winnsboro and all of North Georgia. Each Christmas, sheets of plywood would be pieced together on the Square parking lot. The girls, aged six to sixteen, would clog scenes from The Nutcracker ballet. Oh, it had many of the well-known scenes, the evil Rat King and his rat friends battling Marya and Nicholas, and, of course, the courageous Nutcracker. It was something to behold each Winnsboro winter.

Betty insisted she pay the air travel expenses for all, even over an objection by Louise. Betty prevailed, and the group had a splendid Christmas vacation. The trip proved to be a real Jamaican adventure.

June's cousin, who was a chef at an all-inclusive vacation resort, Sugar Hill at Ocho Rios, was able to get the women two rooms at the beach side facility. According to the rules, it was a couples only establishment, but the cousin convinced the owners to make an exception for the ladies. June stayed with her sisters and showed her friends the local sights each day.

The first full day at the resort, June took the

group to a little-known beach near Oracabessa, that she had frequented as a little girl. All the ladies, except Louise, wore island cover-ups, and carried giant bags containing sun block, dark glasses, books and magazines, and the like. Louise wore a batik pants suit bought by Betty at Parisians, before the ladies had left Georgia. Not an inch of Louise's skin was touched by the warm December rays.

The ladies spread their giant towels under a grove of coconut and palm trees and faced the turquoise waters. Martha pulled off a blue, flower wrap-around and relaxed on her towel, her soft auburn hair pulled up in the back and her tiny Texas pendant lying flat on her throat. June, sporting a giant straw hat, removed her pure white terry cloth robe and then sat directly in the sand, running her dark fingers through the crystalline grains. Betty, untied a long, Hawaiian print shirt and folded it neatly to use as a pillow. Heddy strolled to the water's edge and returned to the group remarking on the beauty of June's secret beach. Somewhere, up in the trees on the hillside and unseen, the sound of Ande's flute and percussion music played Christmas tunes which wafted down to the women as a holiday present from a stranger.

Heddy fetched her towel and walked back to the moist sand nearer the water. She stretched out her towel, imprinted with a giant face and bare chest of Burt Reynolds which was now fading with age. Standing, with her back to her closest friends in the world, yet about twenty feet away, she allowed her Mickey Mouse cover up to fall slowly down her back and finally all the way to the towel, like a young movie star seduced by the sea. The removed mouse wrap exposed a chunky, but firm body clad only in an electric neon green thong bikini. Heddy's cheeks hung in the Jamaican air looking like a Japanese summa wrestler. At once, the almost two-hundred pound, five-foot ten-inch red-head let out a war cry and crashed into the still water making echo rings across the isolated cove. The four women chuckled at Heddy's headstrong personality.

That night the ladies went to the home of June's sister and consumed a feast of *moros y christianos*, white rice, red beans, coconut milk, scallions, and island seasonings. The meal was watered down with bottles of Red Stripe Beer; enjoyed by June's family and friends. Before sunset, the group took a short ride to the blue mountains which were covered by thousands of acres of Forget-Me-Not flowers.

The second day of their adventure, June's cousin loaded the five ladies up in a extra-long jeep, the kind used for tourists, and took them to Dunn River Falls, a series of cascades that spanned over five hundred feet. With June's encouragement, Betty, Martha Rae and Heddy followed their Jamaican friend into the falls where they happily splashed water on each other with their feet, while carefully holding hands. Louise, simply sat on a nearby rock, refusing to go near the refreshing water.

Later, the five pilled back in the jeep and the driver took them to the Rio Grande River. There, they boarded a flat raft and floated down the eight mile river. June, Betty and Martha sat in the front. Heddy in the middle, with Louise in the back, just in front of the "captain," who used a long bamboo pole to help push and guide the craft down the lazily moving stream. The man was a powerfully-built sleek, young Jamaican who ran his own independent rafting operation. He wore green and white striped shorts, no shirt, and a red and white fur Santa hat. After all, it was Christmas.

The captain, named Phillipe, was a real character. He sang and told stories all along the way, making the front four ladies cry with laughter; Louise looked like she just wanted to cry. She sat there, in the back, rarely making a sound or displaying any other facial expression other than a set of quivering lips.

After a while, Phillipe noticed Louise's lack-luster personality. He had been smoking what the locals called "wacky-weed." Out of an act of generosity, he offered his closest customer a puff, not knowing she enjoyed smoking. Without any hesitation, and wishing for a smoke, Louise took what appeared to her to be a hand-rolled cigarette and inhaled a rather long, and much needed, drag. Louise was a long-time "Lucky Strike" smoker and welcomed the offer. Phillipe, with a quick smile, recaptured the joint from

Louise and again took a puff on his wacky-weed.

In no time at all, Louise's eyes became watery and she cocked her head to one side, releasing smoke from her lungs, through those curiously twitching, yet still pursed lips. He continued to sing and offered her the cigarette once more and again she smoked. Within minutes, her famous lips finally relaxed and something happened that hadn't happened in many years, a smile. A small, sweet smile.

The beautiful dark man, kind of a Jamaican Santa Claus, was slowly breathing life into a lifeless Louise. Phillipe sang a smooth song about a plantation overseer who made love to his mistress in a local mansion. Soon, with a constant dance of the weed in her mouth, the faint smile turned to an *audible* giggle, thus alerting the raft-mates on the bow to the miraculous events on the stern. Hearing the strange giggle, the other four women turned in unison to see Louise Patton's wrinkled face aglow with happiness.

"Loooou?" Heddy slowly said, sounding like a tire losing air. "Are you OK?"

Louise continued laughing and joined Phillipe on the chorus of the love song, erasing decades of hard facial lines and astonishing all on board. Phillipe, covered with beads of sparkling sweat, just kept on pushing the bamboo cane and singing, keeping his mischief a secret.

As the raft came to the end of the journey and the ladies climbed back on the dock, Phillipe handed

Louise, secretly in a closed fist, another "cigarette" and wished her a merry Christmas and happy New Year. The others were totally unaware and bewildered as they walked back to the jeep. Louise just smiled.

After sunset, the ladies attended a beach party on the sandy beach at the resort. Louise lagged behind, while the other four went ahead. At the room, Louise lit the "gift" and smoked every shred, thinking it to be some kind of tropical cigarette, and not realizing it was marijuana. Once the joint took effect, Louise put on an island sarong Betty had bought at the Coconut Grove Plaza shopping area.

Feeling most unlike herself, Louise headed for the beach party to join her friends who were intently watching a group of dancers dancing to reggae music. Her friends were amazed to see Louise dressed in the outfit, which exposed a large portion of her lily white shoulders. Louise just smiled at her friends. Soon, Limbo poles were brought out and the band played the customary Limbo song, to which Louise jumped right in. Looking like it was as usual as opening her briefcase, Louise took it right down to the bottom setting, her thin body slipping well under the pole. Her friends cheered. The crowd loved this woman who seemed so set-free from the boundaries of life. Neither Louise or her friends knew the true source of her new found freedom. During the last two days, Louise insisted she and her friends re-visit the rafting man named Phillipe. But they didn't. On the seventh day of their Christmas trip, the Funeral Club left the blue Jamaican mountains and returned to the Blue Ridge Mountains of North Georgia. Louise never seemed so relaxed and happy as she did during that holiday. Her personality returned, which probably explains why she did what she did after that letter arrived.

Adjusting her trifocals, Louise, seated in her office, opened the briefcase. She took out the letter and re-read it carefully. The Loemann & Loemann offer seemed the best way to bring the history of Hunt & Larkin to a suitable end. There was no need for emotional pangs. It was a good offer and the alternative, competition from a big city funeral home, would mean Betty would be left with nothing but a broken down building. Louise reached for the black phone and dialed. Someone on the other end promptly answered.

"Loemann & Loemann. How may I direct your call?"

CHAPTER FOUR

Y ou have to understand that Louise was not at all a bad individual. She was perhaps the one reason Betty had all the money she needed for the rest of her life, no matter what was to happen to Hunt & Larkin. Louise knew how to do three things very well: (1) make lots of money, (2) spend very little money, and (3) draw her mouth up in that tight, funny little position.

One of the worst arguments the ladies ever experienced centered around Louise and followed the loss of Imogene Jackson, the hair dresser who styled the hair of most all the women clients and some of the men at Hunt & Larkin. It was actually the *replacement* of Imogene that caused the disagreement.

Following her divorce and a local church incident, Imogene moved to Columbus with her five fat-faced kids. The children came by their "heartiness" from mom, naturally. Imogene weighed about two-hundred, seventy-five pounds and could single-handedly maneuver just about any client into the appropriate position for her "do."

Imogene had been physically abused by her husband, Royce, over the years and normally saw the confrontations as her own fault, even though they weren't. She was a large woman filled to the brim with unwarranted guilt. Her outlet for the self-condemnation was church. Imogene had been a member of the Winnsboro Methodist Church for years, but sought the piety of the Return Holiness Congregation Church minister, following yet another undeserved beating from Royce.

The meeting with the minister "took" and soon she and the kids started attending the spirit and music filled congregation. In no time, Imogene and her children decided to join the church. Since their Methodist baptism was only a sprinkling, a method not recognized in the Return Church, they would have to face the plunge.

Following the invitational hymn one sweltering Sunday morning (the Church did not have air conditioning), the hefty family positioned itself in front of the altar during the last verse of "Washed in the Blood of Jesus." The minister directed all six out the side door, near the pecan colored pulpit, and into a room to prepare for their baptism. Because the minister was recovering from a bad summer cold, he retuned to the sanctuary and stood on the choir side of the baptismal font. The font was separated from the bass section of the choir loft by a low rising, lime green glass panel. The preacher rolled up the sleeves of his starched monogrammed shirt. He placed himself just behind the last row of chairs in the bass section and prepared for the first Jackson, hoping to reach over and submerge the sinners as they drifted from right to left.

Each of the Jacksons were instructed by Miss Pomproy, the ladies circle leader, to enter a small anteroom, remove their clothing, and put on a white plastic robe. They were to leave their clothing behind with Miss Pomproy who would take the clothing to the other side of the font via a back passage way. Once the baptism was complete each person could re-dress behind a folding screen which also hid a stack of white towels for drying off.

First, eleven year old Terri, the youngest Jackson, walked up the cold concrete steps and gracefully took the minister's hand as he reached over the thick glass wall. She slipped into the water and held his hairy hands tightly as he took the child beneath the cool water with a slight shock. The Reverend seemed a little awkward as he attempted to not turn full-back to the congregation, instead keeping his body perpendicular to the smiling flock of onlookers.

Next, the thirteen-year-old twins, Tracey and Tonya, two plump pumpkin bookends, splashed as they followed quickly behind Terri. The two smiled gleefully as they floated along like twin fishing bobbins, taking their turns being pushed slightly below the water's surface as if being tugged by a large fish, perhaps whale.

Fifteen-year-old Travis, weighing in at over two-hundred, twenty-five pounds now drifted toward the minister trying desperately to keep his plastic gown tightly plastered next to his flabby body. Moments earlier, Miss Pomproy had told him to remove his clothing and so he did, underwear and all. Under the plastic robe, which angelically drifted away from his floating body, the boy was understandably naked. It was obvious to all in the congregation that he didn't want the preacher, or anyone, to see anything or any part. The minister winced as the boy teetered in the water causing the level to rise and fall. Travis was dunked briefly and the water neared the top of the glass, spotting the minister's white shirt at the waist line, just above his belt. As Travis climbed up the short flight of concrete steps to exit the pool, the once wandering plastic robe now clinging to his porkish wet body like plastic wrap, which he was trying to pull *away* so that Miss Pomproy, standing there with his clothing, would not see the outlines of any of his various body parts.

Teresa, a giant sugar plum, launched herself into the spiritual bath like a grand new ship at sea. Before the minister could move his feet, which were sporting new glassy black shoes, a small tide of aqua water lapped over the glass divider, causing the preacher to jump slightly and several members of the bass section to look around embarrassingly. No one in the choir loft dared move, however, to keep from distracting from the seriousness of the spirit-filled service. Teresa went under in a nose dive and surfaced near the steps, by-passing the preacher all together. As she stepped out she saw a hand painted sign above her which read, "TO SERVE." It was now Mama Jackson's turn to be washed up, scrubbed with the sacred waters of the cement pool.

Imogene slid carefully into the water trying her best not to make waves, something she tried to do most of her life. Unfortunately, she had been a more than adequate model for her children in gaining weight. She had watched how perilously close the water had come to spilling with each child's passing. She decided the best approach was to simply float calmly near the middle of the long, narrow bath. Imogene was a little too far from the minister as she floated near the middle of the baptistry. The Jackson matriarch dog-paddled briefly, underneath the water's surface, hoping to back up and become more even with the man in the crisp white shirt, dry vest, and trousers. She held out her soft pink hand as if to seek God's hand for steadfastness. Unfortunately, it was one of God's right-hand men, not himself, who grabbed Imogene Jackson. Briefly, the duo danced back and forth, he in the air, she in water, as members of the bass section swayed slightly left and right, hoping to escape the possibility of the preacher tumbling over into their laps. All were wishing for a miracle, that an angel would leap down from the stained glass window above the baptistry to steady God's servant and his new found sheep, bringing her to a safe and calm landing on God's steps just a few strokes away. The angel didn't move, not one inch. Instead, the winged, naked figure in the colorful cut glass smiled down at the scene as if to be amused by the possibilities.

The minister, already visibly shaken by the whole affair and slightly damp from previous passings, struggled to let go of the biggest fish he had ever caught. Finally, as if pulled through the air by his hand-to-hand joining with Imogene, the preacher toppled over into the tank, head first, as Imogene's legs, arms, and plastic robe thrashed in the sacred waters. It was a sight to behold. Those left abandoned in the congregation didn't know whether to laugh, cry, or pray. They mostly just sat and stared in disbelief, hoping someone would just draw the red velvet curtain fastened at each side of the baptistry.

The choir ran from their brown metal folding chairs as the minister splashed, causing water to overflow by the gallons into the loft. The preacher held on to the slick glass wall with one hand, his shiny black shoes kicking the green water near the bottom, and his other hand firmly clasping the backside of Imogene's plastic robe. He gave her a gentle pushy-push which sent her to the steps, after having gone under several times too many, but surely cleansed throughout. The choir director closed the service with a quick prayer as the minister made his way out of the tank, his black silk suit plastered to his body, heading for his office and shaking off the wetness from his soggy clothes like a pet emerging from an unwanted bath.

The fat family finished drying, dressing, and drove straight home. Sadly, a few days later, Imogene, humiliated and embarrassed, packed all their posses-sions and moved her family to Columbus where her mother lived. While a somewhat funny, or at least shocking affair, it was still sad to see Imogene face years of problems with Royce, topped by the botched baptism. Her husband had failed her, the church had failed her, in general, life had failed her. After she left, no one in Winnsboro ever heard from Imogene again. That presented a real problem for Hunt & Larkin because no one, absolutely no one, could do dead folks' hair like Imogene. No one even wanted to do dead folks' hair. No one, until June.

June volunteered to do hair until a replacement could be found. She loved to do hair and could do it surprisingly well for someone who had never been to cosmetology school. In Jamaica, June would do all her sisters' hair and even her brothers' when theirs got really long. Of course, she did not share Louise's passion for thrift. After her first week of adding hair fixin' to her duties, she ordered several boxes of supplies from a beauty supply house in Gainesville, toward Atlanta. Four-hundred dollars worth, to be exact. It was perhaps the tightest anyone had ever seen Louise's little lips.

June bought the most expensive shampoos, conditioners, rinses, and perms. She purchased a whole line of fingernail polishes and several boxes of brushes, combs, and eye lash pluckers. June was ready for farewell make-overs.

Before Louise discovered the newly acquired beauty products, June thought a whole new career had opened up for her. Shortly after the boxes of stuff arrived, so did Mrs. L.D. McBride. While Heddy was out for lunch, June propped up the body of the eighty-one-year-old Mrs. McBride in a Naugahyde easy chair Heddy kept in the prep room. It was there for Heddy to relax in (out-of-sight) while waiting for the next client to arrive.

Mrs. McBride, already embalmed, was sitting in the easy chair with several wooden cola crates under her, to bring her head up above the back of the dark green plastic vinyl. June had never done hair with the person lying flat on a table and so adjustments were in order. She wrapped three layers of gray duct tape completely around the old lady and the chair to hold the body in the correct position. Once Mrs. McBride was stable, June reached over to a table radio, normally tuned to the local station for news, and switched it on, tuning it to an Atlanta station.

Her favorite station played "oldies" which reminded her of back home when she would buy used eight track tapes of American music, which she played on a small stereo. June sang along.

"...different strokes, for different folks...so on, and so on, and scoo-be-do-be-do!

I...I...I...love everyday people!"

Mrs. McBride, her eyes glued shut and appearing comfortably relaxed, seemed to enjoy all the post-mortem attention so thoughtfully heaped on her by the Jamaican mortician turned beautician. Sly Stone was one of June's favorite performers. He had been to Jamaica for several concerts and she had seen him live!

June adjusted the yellow chiffon dress Mrs. McBride was now wearing, pulled the lever on the easy chair and gave her a fresh blue hair rinse by leaning the head over the sink. After curlers and blow dryer, June propped the woman back to a sitting position. Her gums had been wired shut so she didn't have to worry with the chin dropping, but her head refused to sit up straight. Finally, at her wits end and needing to apply the face make-up and finish the hair, June simply cut a hole in the bottom of a discarded grocery box and slipped it upside down over Mrs. McBride's shoulders. The old lady sat there erect, her head perched on top of an upside down Del Monte green bean box with June now lip syncing the words to "The Lion Sleeps Tonight." With June taking the low bass parts, one might have expected, at any moment, for Mrs. McBride to burst in with the high melody.

Unexpectedly, though, it was Heddy who burst in...the back door. Heddy's eyes fell upon June who was now holding Mrs. McBride's right hand, tenderly, and painting a fine coat of Blossom Red polish on the stained nails. June looked up at Heddy and exulted:

"Boo noo noo noos!"

"And Boo noo noo noos to you too, both of you!" countered Heddy.

A few days later, Louise roared into Betty's office with the hair supply bill, which she had received in the mail, and demanded an explanation. Betty didn't know anything about it. Louise headed straight for the prep room. Poor June. It was a time for tight lips.

"What the hell is this?" Louise blasted, shaking the pink invoice in her pale clenched fist.

June, in her humorous way, probably said the absolute worst thing she could have.

"Loose lips sink ships."

Louise burst back through the door and screeched to a stop at Betty's desk.

"Fire her!"

"Who?" Betty asked

"June. Fire her, now! She spent four-hundred

fifty dollars on a bunch of hair garbage that we don't need. *Fire her, fire her damnit!*"

"Louise, please calm down."

"I won't calm down until you fire her." Louise flew out, slamming the front door so hard that the Palladian window shook. Betty, still sitting at her desk, sighed, stood up and went back to the prep room. June was now standing at the counter, straightening her newly purchased make-up items.

"I think she's mad," June confessed.

"Yes," Betty replied, wanting more information.

"I was just trying to help."

"What exactly is it that we bought?" Betty asked quietly.

Together they looked over the supplies and Betty listened attentively while June explained the need for each item. After a few minutes Betty reached over for June's hand and told her not to worry about anything. She didn't.

Betty went back to her desk and called Louise at home. The answer came on the first ring, as if she were sitting next to the old black dial phone.

"Louise we need to talk."

"There's nothing to talk about, all you have to do is fire her," Louise still fumed.

"Lou, we do not have a hair dresser right now. We aren't spending a single dime to have the service provided for the clients. No one in this town will help us out. June is very excited about this new responsibility. She made old Mrs. McBride look like a Starsearch Spokes Model. You know, in most funeral homes it's some strange man who puts makeup on the women clients. June went the extra mile and did something few morticians in this entire state would do. She gave a personal touch. She gave Mrs. McBride and her family something very special. Relax."

"Look, I have been responsible for the money end of this business for over forty years. If you don't want me to continue, just tell me."

"Louise, I want you to continue. But we're in a bind. Do you want to pay someone to drive up from Gainesville to do hair? Now that will be real cheap. Yes, four-hundred fifty dollars is a lot of money. If a hair dresser comes along who is willing to do dead folks' hair, we'll return any unopened items. If not, we'll use them."

"Fine, fine. Just fine. I don't understand why we can't buy cheaper brands at the new Mega-Mart. You know cheap shampoo by the quart or something."

"Louise, we can, *next time*, ok?" Betty said soothingly as possible.

The phone went click in Betty's ear. Louise had hung up without saying good-bye. In almost fifty years she had never done that. It was almost a week before Louise called or came back to Hunt & Larkin. Betty honestly thought it was all over. When pay checks were due, however, she arrived. June came timidly out of the prep room and immediately apologized for the "lip" remark, but Louise failed to acknowledge the apology or even June's presence. June tried a second time.

"Ms. Louise, I really am sorry for making an ugly comment to you. Really."

Louise just sat there looking over the pay checks and then admitted, in spite of herself, "Fine. Fine." And that was all she said before leaving. It was a long time before Louise and June could really talk again. The cold shoulder lasted months. It's hard to believe that Louise could have been so angry about the make-up. Perhaps it was situations like the "make-up affair" that explain why Louise called Mr. Kline.

From the other end of the line, the business voice answered.

"Mr. Kline speaking."

"Yes, this is Louise Patton. I am the bookkeeper for Hunt & Larkin Funeral Home. We just received your letter."

"Oh, that's good. Then you are interested?"

"Perhaps."

"Tell me Ms. Patton, uh, may I call you Louise?"

"I suppose," the raspy voice reluctantly agreed, not wanting to give up ground.

"Louise, we really are interested in purchasing Hunt & Larkin. It would be a great investment for a regional funeral home chain based in South Georgia, and it would be a tremendous business deal for Mrs.

Larkin. If there is any way you could persuade her to sell, it would be a benefit to all concerned."

"Maybe, maybe not." Louise retorted ambiguously.

"How's that?"

"Mr. Kline, while Betty Larkin and I are financially secure, there are three other women here who are not. They have worked for Mrs. Larkin for many years. One, our mortician, has been with the business since the 1940's. Two others have been with Mrs. Larkin for shorter periods of time, but have little, if any retirement benefits. If you bought the home, what would happen to their jobs?"

"In all candor, Louise, the purchasers could not guarantee them their jobs. We would help them, if possible, but they may be out of luck. They are not executives, you understand. There is a possibility that the current facility, particularly in its present state, would be leveled, or sold, and a new, more modern funeral home would be built at the cemetery...or perhaps out on the bypass. Are you familiar with the area out on the bypass?

A long silence.

"Yes, I am," Louise responded slowly.

"Well, of course no one really knows what would happen until after the sale. And, if we can't get Mrs. Larkin to agree to the offer, out investor may go ahead and build a new funeral home and, well, as the bookkeeper for Hunt & Larkin, you know what that would mean."

"Yes, I am afraid I do."

"Well?"

"How soon do you need a response from us?" Louise asked.

"Soon. Very soon."

"May I suggest you come visit us, the week after next, say November 7th? Could you wait until then?" Louise proposed while flipping the opened left lock on her briefcase.

"Yes, I suppose. I'll be there on the 7th."

"Thank you, Mr. Kline," Louise added and hung up the phone. She sat there quietly looking at a desk calendar. Then she picked up a pen and wrote "Kline 10 A.M." on the space for November 7th.

Louise looked out the small office window that faced up the street toward the funeral home. In the distance she could barely make out the tops of the long row of maple trees. The wind was blowing more swiftly now and the orange and red leaves at the top of the trees were flying off in many different directions. A few totally bare branches at the tree tops were visible.

.

C H A P T E R   F I V E

There was a solid knock on the outside prep room door. Heddy jumped from her easy chair and yanked twice before the stubborn door unlatched. The door swung open and there stood a delivery man. A *new* delivery man.

"Have a box for you on the truck, looks like it might be, you know, one of those, uh, you know..."

"Casket? Casket! It's called a casket!" Heddy muttered.

Heddy helped the delivery man unload the large box and placed it in the garage because the prep room had a "client" in it.

"Thanks."

"Yeah." Heddy barely conceded.

Heddy popped the staples out of the box and pulled back the heavy cardboard. Inside was a gleaming white coffin with brass trim. Hunt & Larkin always kept a dozen caskets in the selection room and the current funeral would require a replacement. As Heddy turned to leave, she noticed a baseball size dent in the front left corner of the coffin.

"Shit," she grumbled, exasperated.

She ran out of the garage and down to the corner to see if she could catch the delivery truck. The driver was just turning right, in front of the maple trees, and Heddy took off after him.

"Hey, stop! Stop, you fool."

The truck backfired and continued on.

"Hey, you bastard. Stop. Hey! Hey!" Heddy slowed down, gasping for air. She was strong, but running after a truck at age fifty-nine, was too much, even for Heddy Hedford. She came to a complete stop and leaned against the last of the maple trees. Heddy crunched underfoot some of the brown leaves that had lain on the ground. She looked up just in time to see Louise coming toward her.

"Morning Louise," Heddy puffed.

"Jogging?"

"No, I was, oh well, yeah, I was," she decided not to reveal the reason for her breathlessness.

"Heddy, by the way, I got a call from the high school wrestling team. They want to borrow a casket for a Halloween project, something about raising money for, I don't know, something."

"Borrow, a <u>casket</u>?"

"Yes."

Louise resumed walking briskly toward Hunt & Larkin. Heddy was following close behind, still panting slightly.

"Hey, I know, a casket came this morning and there is a big dent in it. It's not usable, we'll have to send it back. What about that one? What about the one with the dent in it, Louise?"

"It doesn't matter to me. Let them have their pick of the lot."

"Louise? Is that you, Louise?" Heddy asked, puzzled by the abrupt change in attitude of the bookkeeper.

While Louise crossed the front lawn of Hunt & Larkin, Heddy cut across the side lawn of the funeral home and entered the building from the back, the prep room door still wide open from her exit.

Heddy hadn't been that surprised at anything since Charles Nickles disappeared in his casket. Nickles, a 1978 client, was a midget and a victim of lung cancer. The man's family did not want him buried in a youth casket. They insisted on a full-sized, adult coffin, even though he was only thirty-seven inches tall.

After the preparation, Mr. Nickles was placed in the left side (head-end) of the large casket, his shoes clearly visible. When the time came to move the casket to the Church of Christ, Heddy lowered the lid and wheeled the long and shiny coffin to the hearse, loading it as usual. The Church of Christ porte-cochere was approached by way of a sloping drive-way.

Heddy pulled the casket out of the hearse, carefully positioning it on the chrome church truck, and wheeled it to the narthex. As usual, Betty requested the congregation to stand, and down the aisle rolled Mr. Nickles's gold metallic casket. When Heddy opened the lid, the man had disappeared! Gone! Absolutely gone! Startled, Heddy looked wide-eyed at Betty, and cleared her throat. She stared at Betty and then flashed her eyes downward.

"What?" Betty lipped softly.

Heddy just slightly shook her head, "No," and looked down at the empty casket. Betty approached the coffin while Heddy stood there mortified. Heddy knew the gentleman was in the casket when she had closed the lid in the Blue Room. It was only a three minute trip to the Church of Christ. Then it hit her. She reached over to the right lid and nonchalantly unhooked the clasp. Heddy slowly lifted the lid. There he was. The little man was all the way to the right, his legs crossed tightly, so as to take up only a foot or two of space. The body, resting on satin sheeting, had slipped down into the leg portion of the casket when the hearse pulled up the rather steep approach outside the church.

Betty walked over to the family and explained there was a problem and that the casket would have to be temporarily removed. The man's daughter, who was a normal-sized adult, had already figured out the problem and said there was no need to remove the casket from the sanctuary. She casually said, "It's okay. Just pull him back up. I'm sure he is enjoying it from up above."

From the phone in the prep room Heddy telephoned the high school. Yes, the school secretary learned, there was a casket at Hunt & Larkin that the Winnsboro Wrestling Team could borrow, club members could just come by and pick it up. Friday was Halloween, so any time during the week would be fine, Heddy assured her.

Wednesday afternoon a pickup with four pumped-up boys crammed into the front seat, pulled up outside the funeral home. They told June, who was answering the phone, that they were here to get the casket. June buzzed Heddy and told her some boys would be around back to get the casket with the dent. The boys thanked June very politely and then pulled their truck around back. The white coffin was very carefully loaded and Heddy was thanked politely.

A day later Betty decided to buy candy for Halloween. Because the M. F. Moses store was no longer open, she drove to the Mega-Mart. She parked her Cadillac on the giant asphalt parking lot and went inside. Betty could not believe her eyes. There was the white casket from the funeral home sitting on two saw horses in the entrance area. A poster board with "Thanks to Hunt & Larkin" was taped to one saw horse. A plastic Frankenstein skull sat in the middle of the opened coffin, with a sign crudely taped to the inside of the raised casket lid. It read:

"Throw a quarter into Frankie's mouth and help the Winnsboro High School wrastler's raise matching funds for the Mega-Mart Scholarship."

Betty winced in disbelief. She couldn't accept what she saw. How could they do this? How could they put her casket right out here in public, and of all places, in the Mega-Mart store? She turned on her heels and quickly made her way back to her car. She drove to the Food-Mart, bought her Halloween candy and returned to Hunt & Larkin.

In the days that followed Betty tried to forget what she had seen and where she had seen it. She was happy to help the Wrestling Club and she certainly believed in scholarships. She would have rather given the cost of the casket to the fund rather than to find her casket there in that particular store.

When the casket was not returned soon after Halloween, she asked Heddy to call and see about it. The boys promised to bring it back shortly. They told her they had used it in a haunted house on Halloween night and needed to clean it up.

On Friday morning, November seventh, Martha Rae was getting the morning coffee ready, as usual, and Betty sat at her desk. About fifteen minutes to ten, Louise came in. Heddy was in the prep room with June, cleaning the instruments from a late night case. Louise sat on the leather couch. Betty was on the phone.

Betty, anxious about the errant casket, put her hand over the mouth piece — she was talking to the school secretary — and buzzed for Heddy. Shortly, both Heddy and June came through the prep door, clean, and curious. Betty asked Heddy the name of the boy who had borrowed the casket. As Heddy opened her mouth to give the name, the front door to Hunt & Larkin opened. The five women turned to look at the door.

An older man entered, and shut the door. The eyes of four of the women grew large; Louise's mouth got small. They stared at the older man. The man stared back. Was this a joke?

The man, in his late sixties, looked EXACTLY like Louise. Exactly. Thick, short, gray hair. Tortoise shell glasses. Black briefcase. Pin-striped suit, black wing tipped shoes, and a funny little mouth that was all puckered up. Louise had an unknown *male* twin!

Heddy choked off her laughter and rushed out of the room. She could be heard guffawing back in the prep room for some time. June joined her. More and more laughter drifted from behind the swinging doors.

In what was a short but seemingly endless amount of time the silence in the parlor was broken by muffled laughter from behind the swinging doors. Betty felt extremely awkward and Louise's mouth had shrank so much that she appeared to have no lips at all. Martha Rae, who never, ever said anything sacrilegious whispered, under her breath, "My God." She then picked up the coffee tray and headed for the kitchen not even offering Louise's perfect match a cup of Jamaica's best.

Betty was the first one to break the silence.

"Uh, may I help you?"

"Yes, I am Marcus Kline. Ms. Larkin?

"What? Uh, yes." Betty looked at Louise curiously and squinted, then continued, "Can I help you?".

"Actually, Ms. Larkin, I want to help you. I sent you a certified letter a few weeks ago and I never heard from you. Did you receive the letter? I spoke with Ms. Patton . . . "

"Well. But, I was not...uh..I am really not interested in selling."

"I understand, Ms. Larkin, but you know if you don't sell Hunt & Larkin, it is very likely that another new funeral home will move in and that would be very bad for you."

"Yes Mr. Kline, I understand that, but I am not interested. I really do not know what else we have to talk about." Betty was speaking with slightly more control and with greater self-confidence.

"Ms. Larkin, may I sit?"

"Well, Mr. Kline..."

"Just for five minutes, please?"

"Okay, five minutes."

Mr. Kline sat down next to Louise on the couch. They looked like a matched set of bookends. For a moment, they were both embarrassed. Louise had not said a thing the whole time Mr. Kline had been present. She just kept her mouth drawn as tightly as possible.

"Ms. Larkin," the man said as he turned his head to get a quick look at Louise, "Loemann & Loemann is not a small company. We have offices all over the South: Dallas, Houston, Little Rock, Birmingham. We are giants in the investment business. Your business may have once been important to you and to the town, but we both know things have changed."

He stepped over toward the Palladian window and peered out nervously, then continued.

"Hunt & Larkin has served this community for many years, I'm sure, but all things come to an end. It is better for you to take what you can get, <u>now</u>, and spend the rest of your life enjoying yourself."

"Mr. Kline, suppose I sold Hunt & Larkin. What about my employees?" Betty asked sternly, rising.

"I really don't know. I have a written offer in my briefcase. I think you should take a look at it."

Kline again joined Louise, who remained

absolutely motionless on the couch. He flipped open his briefcase. Retrieving a contract, he handed it to Betty who was still standing. The contract read:

"Loemann & Loemann, Inc., on behalf of South Georgia Funeral Corporation offers the sum of $500,000 to Betty Larkin, for the name "HUNT & LARKIN" and all property, assets and liabilities of the company existing in Winnsboro, Lanier County, Georgia. This offer must be accepted or rejected by December 15, 1991."

Betty saw the words, and slowly slid into the seat behind her desk. She laid the paper down and glanced at the golden leaves floating past the giant Palladian window.

"Ms. Larkin, are you all right?" Kline asked.

"What, oh, yes. Yes."

"Well, I'll leave the offer with you. I'll phone you in a few days. Take care."

The Patton double snapped his briefcase shut, rose and exited officiously from Hunt & Larkin. As the door closed, the staff members entered and converged on Betty. They stood around her looking puzzled. Suddenly, Louise who was still rigidly ensconced on the couch, released her tight little facial muscles and spoke for the first time in fifteen minutes. She said something no one had *ever* heard her say,

"Boo noo noo noos."

CHAPTER SIX

The *Winnsboro Banner* was a weekly news-paper. Its articles almost never covered controversial issues. More often, they reported in detail on the band trip, high school athletic events, and revivals. The week of November 14, all that changed.

When Louise laid the paper on the parlor desk that Monday morning, there was a great banner head-line for all to see.

"HUNT & LARKIN TO CLOSE DOORS."

Betty was irate. "Where in the world did they get this information?"

"Not from me," Louise sat defensively erect in the big chair.

"I don't understand. The man just paid us a visit. I didn't sign anything or give any kind of commit-ment. This isn't fair. I'm calling Harold Prince. No, the editor isn't high enough. I'm calling the publisher. What's that fellows name in Gainesville? Barton, Barkton?"

"Barker. John Barker. But he isn't the publisher any more. They sold the paper to Harold because revenues were down. Don't call him yet. It might be worth your while to find out who leaked the news."

"Leaked the news? Lou, I'm <u>not</u> selling," Betty insisted, softly but emphatically.

Betty picked up the paper and again read the article. To her astonishment, Heddy Hedford was quoted as the source throughout the article. Betty reached over to the buzzer and leaned on it with forceful insistence. Over the small mic, she directed Heddy to come up front. As an afterthought, she added in an annoyed tone, "Please remove your jacket before you come!"

Heddy sauntered into the main room.
"Yes?"

"Heddy, what is the meaning of this?" Betty demanded, thumping the headline.

"Holy Moses, you've decided to sell?"

"No, I realize it says that, but I'm not selling. Why did you tell them this?

I didn't tell them you were selling, I just answered Harold's questions. He promised it was off the record."

"Well, apparently it was not off the record. It's on the record, and all over the front page." Betty was angry and determinedly controlled.

"Betty, let me see it."

"I am quoted three times. I never said anything about you selling, see? All I said was that a man had visited Hunt & Larkin with an offer to buy. Also, here, Harold asked if I would miss working at Hunt & Larkin after forty years and I said 'Of course.' Finally, right here, see, he asked, 'Is Betty faced with selling Hunt & Larkin?' My answer, 'I don't know you'll have to ask Betty.' I don't see anything to get all huffy about. I thought I handled it pretty good. I am angry, though. That bastard, Harold Prince, told me that he wouldn't print my comments, or my name. You want me to call him?"

"No, Heddy. I'm sorry. It's my fault. Go on."

"Betty, I've been here a long, long time. I would never embarrass you, or any of us. Never."

Heddy's eyes darted from Betty to Louise as she headed back to the prep room. Betty remained at her desk, her sparkling blue eyes now filled with tears of exasperation.

"I just don't understand. We just want to run this business. It has been here so long. Why doesn't everyone just leave us alone? Don't they know we can do this a lot better than some anonymous chain organization who will bring in a staff who doesn't know anyone. They won't care about the hurt. The suffering. The tragedies. Death is personal. People are better off when they can struggle with their friends rather than with some total stranger. It's not supposed to be some cold-hearted assembly line affair owned by people far away. It won't be long before funeral homes here are like those insensitive ones in Japan that are in shopping malls, making the death observance of a loved one just another mass market service like cooking hamburgers. What is this country coming to?"

Betty almost broke. Louise watched in silence. A moment later, Betty walked quickly out of the room and out the front door of Hunt & Larkin. Louise waited a couple minutes and then left also. She didn't even notice the few maple leaves that continued to cling to the branches on the lower halves of the trees. Louise followed the sidewalk back to her house.

In the prep room, Heddy was staring at the phone. If her eyes had been laser beams, the phone would have instantly disintegrated. She grabbed the receiver off the hook. The number of the newspaper office had been penciled over the phone to provide the paper with obit information. The long phone cord stretched as Heddy moved, phone in hand, into her easy chair. She leaned back defiantly, and listened as the phone rang in the newspaper office. Finally, someone answered.

"Mr. Prince, please," she managed with altogether too much courtesy.

"Harold Prince."

"Harold. Oh, Harold. This is Heddy Hedford. I just read this morning's paper..."

"Yeah, Heddy..."

"Harold..."

"Yes?"

"Why don't you take a stainless steel mortician's aspirator, and go screw yourself!"

Heddy let go of the receiver and the stretched phone flew across the room, hit the wall and fell to the floor, bouncing around like a run over snake.

Heddy was not someone to have on the opposing team. That she had a mean, obstinate streak was no secret. More than one person had realized, that when confronting Heddy, prompt surrender was the preferred action. Shortly, the large, red-headed woman got up, walked to the phone and replaced it on the hook.

Heddy had come to Hunt & Larkin as a dropout of Winnsboro High School. Her mother was all Irish and her father left soon after she was born. Her birthplace was never officially known, but when asked she would say, "East of the sun, west of the moon." Early in her career, she realized that funeral home work suited her. She trained weekends at the mortuary school in Atlanta during the second year that she worked for Cecil. Heddy started out as a helper, with duties similar to June's. It was so exciting to her that she had talked Cecil into paying her schooling costs in Atlanta. He did. She went.

There was no post mortem case in the world that

would have caused Heddy to lose a breath. Not one. She loved the gore. Once, when a plane crashed at the Atlanta airport, she volunteered her services, not so much to help, but to see what dead, burned bodies looked like. The emergency services gladly accepted her gesture, never imagining what delight it brought to her. She took pictures, too.

Mrs. Hedford had no children but had been married three times. Each time to the same man, Ed Hedford, a plumber. Ed drank excessively. It was his drinking that caused Heddy to leave each time. Otherwise, the two had much in common. Draining pipes and bodies seemed like similar occupations. They both used gadgets and cleaners. They were truly a pair.

Their first divorce was caused by an argument over tools. Ed was working on the plumbing at M.F. Moses and found a clog in a very small drain. It was one of those overflow affairs in the back room of the variety store that was never really used but needed to be there just in case. The drain had a strange opening and Ed couldn't get his normal working tools down into the hole. He was smashed, of course.

Ed sloshed over to Hunt & Larkin and entered by the back door. Heddy had gone out to lunch. He examined all the instruments until he found a long, curved tube that looked as if it would do the job. His body weaved left and right as he headed back to the five-and-dime. The instrument did work just fine.

The drain emptied when he poured a bucket of water down into it. He repacked his tools, but in his drunken state, left the stainless steel tube lying on the floor.

The manager was grateful for the repaired drain, but was perplexed by that surgical looking tube left behind by Ed. She called the town physician who came over and identified it as a mortician's trocar. It was returned to a very angry Heddy Hedford. She confronted Ed, who denied taking it. Heddy probably would have overlooked this had the store manager and the doctor not become involved. But when Ed denied it, in the face of guilt, she divorced him.

About six months later, they remarried. Twice more, they divorced, each time because Ed had done something stupid while under the influence of alcohol. In the end, however, Heddy got the best of Ed. She had said several times, "I hope to hell, when that son-of-a-bitch dies, that we are in the divorce side of our cycle." They were. Ed died from cirrhosis of the liver six months after their last divorce. He had taken Heddy's new custom van and wrecked it one Friday night as he was coming home from a binge in Atlanta. He had spent four hours drinking and drooling over the young female bodies at the Leopard Club, one of the largest strip joints in the Southeast.

As Heddy told the story, she pumped his "rotten fat-assed body" full of lye. In no time flat, the lye would eat up Ed, his cheap casket, and maybe, the bottom of the steel vault. No one could get the upper hand on Heddy. Not even in death.

Heddy used to brag that embalming bodies was like changing the oil in a car. Heddy likened her self to a grease monkey standing by the oil rack in a service station, draining the old and filling with the new. A few squirts of grease here and there, a kick or two to the tires and then you roll 'em out. Even Stephen Davis's death, which touched June and the others, never really phased her. She was as cold and hard as a "frozen town watchmen."

Later, Heddy, dejected about the newspaper article, called upstairs to June and told her she was leaving for the day and to be sure to cover any phone calls. Heddy was the last to leave. Louise and Martha had gone home at the usual hour. Only June remained. The only light visible that evening, in the massive old building, shone in June's bedroom. Outside, it cast an eerie soft yellow glow on the totally bare branches of the maple trees.

C H A P T E R   S E V E N

The next morning, Tuesday, November 15, Betty got up extra early after not being able to sleep all night. She parked her white Cadillac in front of Louise's house. Betty went to the front door and pushed the round black bell button. A few wispy spider webs connected the button and small crevice in the white wood siding. The gray porch was damp from the recent rain and a slight odor of mildew was discernible.

A light went on in the living room and the over-sized, leaded glass door opened.

"Hi, Lou. Let's talk."

"Come in."

"I won't stay long."

"Have a seat."

"No, I need to make some calls and I have some

other errands to run. I've thought about this all night and I know what I want to do."

"Yes."

"Lou, I want you to have some legal papers drawn up."

"You've decided to give in?"

"No, not at all."

"I want you to have a lawyer draw up some papers, giving each one of us twenty per cent ownership of Hunt & Larkin."

"My God, are you crazy?"

"Yes. Probably."

"Betty, I don't think this is a good idea. They are offering you a lot of money. A whole lot! I mean, why in the world would you..." They both sat.

"Please don't try to talk me out of it. We both know I have enough money to do whatever I wish to do the rest of my life. So do you. But the other girls in our little Club do not. If we are going to close down, I want each of them to make the decision to do so. I won't have to feel responsible in any way. If they vote to close, fine, they will each have one-fifth of the $500,000 offer. That will go a long way to help each of them. Neither of us really needs the money and you know that... Lou, quit making that awful shape with your lips. PLEASE."

"Betty, you have worked very hard. Indeed, I have worked very hard, fifty-one years to be exact. I am not sure this is the smart thing to do. This is your business and you should sell it, take the revenue and go off somewhere. You will never realize this kind of a profit from Hunt & Larkin in the remaining years of your life. You should take advantage of a very good business offer. Look, it's not my money or my business, and it certainly doesn't belong to Martha, Heddy or June. It's yours."

"Yes. It's mine. And that's why I am doing what I want to do with it. Ok? Please just have the legal paper work drawn up before Christmas, so I can give all three of them, and you, a little surprise. Ok?" There was a long silence as the two sat, staring in different directions.

"Ok, I'll do it. It's against my better judgment, but I'll do it."

"Fine, see you a little later."

Betty got up, leaving a clean spot in the dark vinyl chair in which no one had sat in recent memory. Neither of them noticed. She got into the car, put it in reverse and backed up the entire two blocks. She parked under the maple trees in front of the funeral home. Betty unlocked the front door and went inside to make coffee.

Louise picked up the phone and called attorney Tom McBride, grandson of Mrs. L.D. McBride, and explained Betty's request. Tom said he would need some more legal information, but would have the papers ready within two weeks. He probably wouldn't though. He always put things off. Louise said she would pick the papers up December 5, and not a day later.

Betty loaded four scoops of ground Jamaican coffee beans into the white paper coffee filter. She added two teaspoons of vanilla to the water and then poured the water into the top of the coffee maker. The vanilla was June's secret touch that the Club had adopted. The brew began to percolate. The aroma quickly rose into the air, and for an instant, in the kitchen, replaced the carnation odor.

Betty went to her desk and began looking at her small desk calendar. She marked December 20 with a big "happy smile."

The newspaper of the previous week lay folded tightly on her desk. Betty opened and spread out the newspaper trying to make the wrinkles lie flat. Once again, she read the "Hunt & Larkin To Close Doors" article. Disgusted, she began turning the pages, each time trying to flatten the wrinkles so the paper would become smooth again. She read about several marriages, a young man who was promoted in the Navy after returning from a recent foreign skirmish, and the local winter festival sponsored by the elementary school.

Betty had helped with the winter carnival almost every year. She worked at the festival because they needed extra adults to assist with all the excited children. She was always willing to work in any booth, and in recent years, had a special booth all her own. In addition, she furnished all the little trinkets given as prizes. This annual event gave Betty an opportunity to have children for an evening.

Several years ago, she convinced Heddy, June, Martha Rae, and Louise to stand behind a tall partition, which was painted on the front side with elaborate ocean waves. Children on the wave side would "cast" small plastic fish poles, and the empty fishing lines would propel themselves through the air, landing behind the partition next to the ladies. Each woman would quickly affix a small prize to the empty hook and then gently pull on the line. Smiles would flash on the children's faces as they reeled in their "catches." It had been the most popular booth at the winter festival from the beginning. It had probably given more joy to the ladies than to the children. Seeing these smiling youngsters brought tremendous happiness to Betty who had always wanted children, but never had any.

As Betty perused the article about the winter festival, she thought about the ways in which Hunt & Larkin had touched the lives of those in Winnsboro. She thought about the Davis boy, old Mr. Morgan, and Mrs. McBride. She thought about thousands of families who had depended upon her and Cecil over the years. She felt a personal attachment to the community, a very solid bond. It was a moral bond that deserved giving the best service available. It was a responsibility that Betty had accepted with great trust from the community. She thought further about the winter carnival and the laughter and surprise her Club members would bring to the children of Winnsboro. A small solitary tear rolled out her eye, down her cheek and gently splashed on the local news. She turned the damp, rumpled page of the paper to find a giant advertisement.

The two-page spread by Mega-Mart made her feel queasy.

"Men's flannel shirts marked half off. All brands of women's hair spray marked down twenty-five percent. Mega-Mart brand paint, three gallons for the price of two. Today only, while supplies last!"

Undeniably, those two pages were filled with genuine good buys. The lowest price anywhere. All made in America. No doubt about that. This place was THE place to shop. No one else would even think about owning a clothing, hardware, five & dime, or drug store in this small community.

Betty glanced out the window and saw the familiar hand scrawled word CLOSED on the dirty window across the street. She wondered if those working in the paint department at Mega-Mart or Save-Mart really knew as much about mixing house paint as Madison Jones once did. She thought about Fred Copeland filling prescriptions for decades for friends and relatives. She considered how Fred knew just about every ailment and allergic reaction of all Winnsboro's residents. Now, here was this new pharmacist who was rotated into town by the mega-giant for a few months. While polite, he did not know the health background of anyone in the community and was there only until a permanent druggist was willing to relocate in the small town. Betty kept turning to more giant advertisements as she read the paper. Food-Mart had a sale on whole chickens and ground beef, each wrapped in clear plastic and possibly injected with who knows what.

In her mind's eye she saw each of the former downtown businesses, Jones' Hardware, M.F. Moses and Copeland's Drug Store. She thought of Grogan's and the care the owners gave to fresh meats wrapped in that white waxed paper.

She wondered if the owners of these former downtown stores were at Mega-Mart, Save-Mart and Food-Mart that very morning. She visualized those owners standing in crowded register lanes, inching loaded baskets toward the scanning registers. They were buying up these fantastic sales and sending off their local dollars to pay the salaries of unknown business managers and executives in some other, more fortunate community, located clear across the country.

Betty squeezed the black and white nightmare together, like an accordion, and stuffed the sorry statement into her trash can. The idea of what had happened to Winnsboro made her physically ill. The problem, not only for Winnsboro but all small communities, seemed so clear. Cut out the middle buyer, buy products at bulk cost from the manufacturer, and stock thousands of stores. Design each and every store to appear the same. Use the same architectural drawings, train the managers in a central location, and connect the entire system by computer and satellite. Where in God's name had small town identity gone? How could anyone stay in business against such odds? The greed seemed overwhelming and visible, not only in big cities, but now in small communities, like Winnsboro all over the country.

The Donna Reed spirit, her trade mark for so many years had gradually disappeared. Her hair even seemed whiter now. Her hands, which almost never shook, shook slightly as she thought about her beloved community. She wasn't even able to make it to the bathroom before collapsing in tears.

Several evenings later while working late, Betty fell asleep on the long sofa in front of the Palladian window. She was awakened about 8:30 the following morning by loud voices outside the funeral home. She glanced out the antique window and there stood half a dozen people chanting and holding signs that read,

"Don't forget Winnsboro! Don't ditch our loved

ones! Keep Hunt & Larkin open! Don't sell out, Betty!"

After reading the *BANNER* article, some of the local townspeople had decided to stage a protest. They were angry at Betty, thinking she wanted to end the business. Of course, they were angry for no reason.

Betty knelt on the sofa, which faced away from the window. She peered over the back of the sofa at the scene outside. She couldn't believe that the people had the story all wrong. Closing was the last thing she wanted to do. As she crouched, backwards on the sofa, Heddy came in from the prep room. Excitedly, she pointed toward the street.

"Hey, did you see what's going on out in front? They're having some kind of protest out there. Did we bury the wrong person or something?"

"Shh, no, it looks like they want to bury me. Maybe us. Just take a look at those signs."

Heddy joined Betty on the couch and squinted to see the signs. She read out loud.

"Our families deserve better. Don't sell."

"Looks as though we have met the enemy and we are she," Betty whispered.

June walked into the main room and caught a glimpse of the two rear ends sticking up in the air.

"Boo noo noo..."

The women hushed her and motioned for her to

join them. Seconds later Martha Rae ventured down the side walk from her parking spot on the Square. Most people knew sweet Martha very well, but they weren't being very pleasant as she passed.

"Tell Betty to go suck an egg," someone shouted.

"Go ahead, turn off the last light in downtown," another taunted.

Martha Rae, carefully holding a newspaper clipping, raced to the front porch steps, past a photographer, and slipped inside. She quickly shut the door, held tightly to the door knob as she imagined a nasty stalker on the other side (though, in fact, no one had dared follow her). The other ladies motioned her to the couch. She crawled toward the large Victorian sofa on her knees. Now, four of the Club members had lined up on the couch, all peaking over the back like shy little animals keeping watchful eyes on their predators. Soon, several dozen more townspeople joined in the secretly planned demonstration, filling the sidewalk from one maple tree to the other. Little did these irate neighbors guess that Betty was actually on their side.

"Enough is enough," Betty finally announced to herself. She grabbed the arm of the sofa to steady herself and rose determinedly. Back straight, steps firm, she went straight for the front door. An age-spotted hand grasped the antique door knob. She paused a second to focus her eyes. The other three ladies crowded behind her. When she stepped outside, most of the people fell silent, but a few continued shouting ugly remarks. Betty attempted to speak,

"You KNOW I don't want to sell Hunt & Larkin..."

A lady yelling at the back interrupted her, but Betty did not lose her concentration.

"But there are some outsiders, people who don't live in Winnsboro, who would like to close us down and buy us out. We are really up against the wall. Thank you for wanting us to continue, but I, we, are not the culprits."

With that, Mrs. Larkin left the porch, turning away from the suspicious crowd, not realizing that this event was just a hint of what was to come. Her three loyal Club members circled protectively around her and followed her inside the funeral home. Many of the people seemed puzzled. Some did not believe Betty. They felt she had just wanted to close the business, make some money, and kiss everyone goodbye. That wasn't the truth.

Betty ached to let Heddy, June, and Martha Rae in on her plan to give them each twenty per cent of ownership. She would wait and follow her plan to present legal papers, wrapped in pretty Christmas paper. This was not the right time.

Martha Rae, always eager to help her friends, volunteered to serve the morning coffee. In the kitchen she fixed a tray and returned to the main parlor. The four sat there discussing the demonstration and wondering who had instigated the incident. Several names were mentioned, but they all agreed it had to be either Mr. Kline or editor Harold Prince. As they talked, Martha remembered.

"Oh, speaking of newspapers, look what my brother in Texas sent." She sprang from the sofa and grabbed the news article, which she had placed with her purse near the front door.

"It's from the *San Antonio Post*, Sunday business section." Handing the small clipping to Betty, Martha continued by reading the headline aloud, "Dallas Firm Investigated Over Real Estate Scheme."

Sitting at her desk, Betty read the second paragraph aloud to her friends. "The Dallas investment firm of Loemann & Loemann is under investigation by the Texas Attorney General's Office for fraud involving massive land purchasing around Garza Lake. The well known regional development group purchased undeveloped land at bargain prices, inflated the value to almost double the original price and then resold the land in package deals to builders."

"These same naughty boys, or their cousins, are up to no good in the Lone Star State," Martha interrupted. Betty finished reading the article as the ladies sipped their morning coffee. The women were facing Goliath, an evil giant that well might be the death of their business. Armed with ammunition, the Funeral Club discussed the possibilities.

The following Monday, the latest issue of *THE*

BANNER lay waiting in all the mail boxes. Louise dropped off the mail and spread the front page across Betty's desk. A picture of the demonstrators was prominently displayed there. It merely amused Betty. She glanced at the headline while nursing her usual coffee. It did not alter her plan to collectively allow the five of them to decide the fate of Hunt & Larkin.

Just below the photograph of a man holding a protest sign, there was a smaller article. The smaller headline read,
"City Council to Discuss Mini-Mall Proposal."

The short article discussed a proposal by the firm, Loemann & Loemann, who wanted to bulldoze three square blocks in downtown Winnsboro for a mini-mall. In short, the proposal was to level all the old vacant stores facing the Square in order to create parking and new streets. Among the list of proposed buildings to be razed was Hunt & Larkin.

Betty focused more on the smaller article. Once again, she felt a sinking spell that caused her momentarily to wonder if maybe she should forget her idea and simply sell, as soon as possible, to Loemann & Loemann. It looked as if she were doomed no matter what she did. The community would really like the old downtown area re-vitalized. It would be for the common good of the community. In fact, many residents might think it advantageous to have the funeral home located closer to the cemetery and a new commercial district developed downtown. Unfortunately, such a plan would mean TOTAL loss of local ownership of every square inch of downtown and the surrounding blocks. Betty reflected that the situation was no different than that of foreign investors who had bought giant office buildings around the country, as well as majority stock in major corporations. Obviously, Hunt & Larkin would be sold, relocated and operated by the regional funeral outfit. The one-hundred year old funeral home would go to its own grave and become a memory. A memory like the thousands of those they had buried. A memory like Betty's blonde hair, like Cecil himself, gone, it now seemed so many years.

CHAPTER EIGHT

For once Tom McBride had his work completed on time. He gave Louise five thick envelopes, each containing the appropriate papers for transferring ownership from Betty to each of the Club members.

Louise brought the envelopes to Betty late in the afternoon on December 5. She signed the papers and Louise notarized them.

Whatever her friends decided to do with Hunt & Larkin really didn't matter to Betty. She just wanted them to be happy and secure, whether that meant coming to work each day or having the $100,000 for retirement. What had been her decision, was now theirs.

"This is really going to be the best thing that could ever happen. I know you don't like it, but then you also didn't like it when Cecil gave the 'night watch-man' an all-expense-paid vacation into eternity," Betty teased gently.

"No, I really do not think it's best; but, we must remember, I work for you."

"Lou, we work together, right?"

Louise's lips started to quiver as she squeaked out,

"Right."

Louise left. From a lower drawer of her desk Betty took out some wrapping paper and carefully folded each of the envelopes in the Christmas paper. On each one she carefully inscribed a name: Louise, Martha Rae, June, Heddy, and her own. Below each, she wrote,

"From: The Funeral Club."

Betty lifted the lid from the small, hand-carved mahogany box. Inside this rough wooden container, placed next to the calendar on her desk, she planned to keep the important papers.

The aromatic box, about ten inches wide and six inches deep, was an unusual acquisition for Betty. Some four or five thousand funerals had been handled by Hunt & Larkin since World War II. Occasionally a funeral took place which resulted in unusual senti-mental objects being left behind.

Seven years before, Heddy and June had picked up a man staying at the Winnsboro Motor Lodge, a deceased man that is. The small motel had twenty rooms, each with a tiny carport. Out front a rusting sign with blue neon tubing permanently glowed, "vacancy." It shone brightly even late on Saturday nights when a car or truck was parked in every slot. One Sunday afternoon, Heddy and June were called to the motor lodge to pick up a guest who had died sometime the previous evening. In the carport they found a worn-out Chrysler with South Carolina plates. The motel manager and investigating deputy warned Heddy and June to cover their eyes before entering the room, and then laughed. Of course, Heddy wasn't about to cover her eyes. This was a gal who enjoyed the macabre. Inside the women burst into laughter. There, lying on the bed, naked and face up, was an old man. That, in itself, was nothing unusual. Many people die in the nude. The shock of this case was that the man was not only stripped and dead, he lay there stiff, with a permanent erection.

Lipstick stain was seen on a cigarette in the ash tray, but no evidence of foul play was discovered, just the kind of play normal for this establishment. They loaded the corpse and covered it with the expected white sheet. The body was very thin and flat, but well endowed. The sight reminded June of her girlhood and how she would set up a tent in her mother's living room using only a broomstick and a bed sheet.

As it turned out, the man had had a penile implant and this had apparently become stuck in the "on" position at the hour of his death. Either that, or some-one had inflated the device after his passing. No one ever knew. No one ever wanted to know. Heddy had to call an urologist in Atlanta to determine how to "release" the mechanism. After the embalming, a South Carolina funeral home sent for the body, which had finally appeared more relaxed.

A few weeks later, a hand-crafted butterfly arrived in the mail. It was made from gold wire and was about four inches tall. The note attached to the delicate art work read,

"To Whom Ever, thank you for taking care of Gene, who was found at the Winnsboro Motor Lodge. He was a good man and a wonderful husband. I am sorry he passed away in your community, alone. Even though he was a stranger, you took care of him. I thank you.

Helen"

A year later, Betty fastened the gold butterfly to the lid of the wooden box which came from yet another client. At that time, a funeral was held for a biker named Jimmie Don Askew. Jimmie Don had grown up in Winnsboro and then moved to Miami when he was in his early twenties. He never did very well in either place. In Miami, he bought a Harley-Davidson motorcycle a month after he got a job working at a dog kennel. It was one of those dog boarding homes that kept pampered pets for tourists. Of course, Winnsboro did not have anything like that so it had impressed Jimmie Don enough for him to want to work there.

He contracted the HIV virus from a promiscuous life and died. The gossip around Winnsboro was that he died from some rare disease he obtained while working at the kennel. His mother did not have enough money to pay the transportation fee to return his remains to Winnsboro.

As his immanent death approached, a doctor in Miami phoned Jimmie Don's mother and told her the young man only had a week or two to live. Betty heard about the situation and provided the mother a round trip plane ticket to Miami to be with Jimmie Don. Other townsfolk contributed money to pay for hotel, taxi and meals while the lady stayed by her son's side.

Jimmie Don's mother had been a housekeeper in Winnsboro for twenty years. She was a humble woman who had hard luck her entire life. Her husband died mysteriously in a hunting accident. He had no life insurance. Her youngest child became pregnant twice before age twenty, without marriage. No matter what tragedy currently faced Mrs. Askew, she always handled her cleaning jobs responsibly. In addition to twelve homes, she also kept the Methodist Church clean. No one ever heard the woman complain about her problems, not even once.

Jimmie Don's motorcycle buddies offered to return his body to Winnsboro in the bed of a pick up truck if his mother and authorities approved. The traditional cost to transport the body would have been impossible for the mother to pay, so Mrs. Askew humbly agreed. The county coroner in Miami also gave his permission, warning the bikers,

"As long as he is properly embalmed, I don't care how you take him."

The friends raised enough money to pay for the body preparation and quickly fashioned a crude wooden casket from rough hewn mahogany. This natural coffin, containing the young bearded man, was loaded on a green side-step Ford truck and driven to Winnsboro, followed by thirty bikers, all decked out in leather gear and opaque sun glasses. Mrs. Askew was picked up at the Atlanta airport by Heddy.

Hunt & Larkin happily received the funeral cortege, which arrived at a time when there were no other clients and while Betty and Louise were out of town. Well, you can just imagine. Some of the large group of unshaven bikers stayed at Jimmie Don's mother's house and the rest camped out on the funeral home lawn. They used the bathroom facilities inside and lit a camp fire outside.

Very polite boys, the bikers made friends with Heddy, June and Martha Rae. They even talked Heddy into taking a "spin" around Lanier County on the back of one Harley. The driver, known only as Reese, appeared to be the leader of the pack.

Heddy was so enthralled over her ride on the bike

that she bought one several weeks after the Askew funeral. Like the hearse before it, the Harley motorcycle became her trademark. In time she bought one of those trailers to match and used it to carry home her groceries. She loved the bike and seldom drove the old Dodge. Besides, she never had to worry about locking her keys inside.

Before he left, Reese was so moved by Heddy's friendliness, that he took several pieces of rough mahogany that the coffin had rested upon in the truck, and made a small box. He presented this unusually attractive box to Heddy. She left it for Betty, as possible ammunition in case her boss was unhappy about the unorthodox visitors. In fact, Heddy didn't particularly like sentimental things. Surely a handmade, keepsake mahogany box, of the exact same wood as Jimmie Don Askew's casket, would squelch any negativeness Betty might overhear from towns people. There never was any, and Betty, the eternal diplomat, seemed grateful for the gift. The box held only very special items in the years that followed.

Into the Askew box Betty laid the important envelopes for her friends and replaced the lid adorned with the gold wire butterfly. On each folded paper she carefully taped a maple leaf from the pen holder. Only one leaf was left on the desk. Wearily, Betty shut the box and left for the night.

By five the next afternoon, when Betty had failed to report for the day, Heddy went by to check on her friend. Through the front window she saw Betty crumpled on the living room floor. Heddy looked unbelieving into the window, and breathed to herself,

"Oh my God!"

She banged on the door to determine if Betty were merely sleeping, but Heddy had seen too many of the deceased to allow for hope. A key that all the Funeral Club members knew about lay under a fake rock in the flower bed. Heddy searched anxiously for it, unlocked the entrance and hurried to Betty's side. The second she touched her friend's arm, she realized the truth. Heddy felt a strange tingle down her back and her heart began racing. She backed up, nearly tripping on a foot stool, and picked up the phone from the end table. She called Louise. In minutes, the four women were standing around Betty's lifeless form. The Funeral Club had died.

Louise contacted the coroner, who arrived quickly to announce Betty deceased, most likely from heart failure. Betty's remains were left with the coroner who transferred them to the small morgue at the hospital where he would determine the official cause of death. Sadly, Betty's friends returned to the old funeral home.

Late into the evening they sat quietly around the Palladian window, all but Heddy in tears. Martha Rae, the Club member best at consoling, was the first to express her feelings.

"It's important for us to understand that Betty was more than our leader, or even our boss. She was our friend. She guided us, helping us all to understand the importance of our individual talents, of being servants to the community. She overlooked our faults and made each one of us feel really special."

Louise continued the tribute.

"That's true. But even more important, she made everyone in this town feel special. She had a way of making everything ok, no matter how bad it really was. You ladies probably didn't know this, but a few weeks ago when the wrestling team returned the damaged casket, it was just about ruined with fake blood. I wasn't impressed. Personally, I would have billed the school for the fifteen hundred dollar coffin, especially in light of displaying it in the Mega-Mart. Do you know what she did? She had me write a five hundred dollar check as a donation to the matching Mega-Mart Scholarship Fund. She made people feel good about themselves. She helped our people feel good about the community."

"I don't know why she hired me. I arrived with a suitcase and nothing else," June remembered.

"You arrived with a suitcase...and a smile," Martha Rae gently corrected.

"And some very good recipes," not talented in the kitchen, Heddy was especially thankful for June's cooking.

"Thank you. Thank each of you very much," June sobbed.

Heddy reminisced,

"Louise will remember this, but I don't think June and Martha Rae have ever heard this story. About ten years before Cecil died, he had to have gall bladder surgery. He certainly wasn't female and most likely not fertile, but he was definitely fat, forty and farting."

The four ladies chuckled.

"He had at least three of the five f's of gall bladder disease," Heddy continued. Louise waited for appreciative smiles through tears.

"Anyway, he was in the hospital over a week. The attack occurred after I had left on my second honeymoon with Ed, which was, of course, a waste of time, as you might expect. While Cecil and I were out of commission, a client arrived. It was a small child, a four-year-old girl who had died of encephalitis. The family had little money and spoke only Spanish. I'm not sure they were legal citizens. To make a long story short, Betty had to embalm the toddler. It was against the law, I'm sure, but she didn't have much of a choice. Before that, she had never come back to the prep room. That was mine and Cecil's turf.

"Betty tried to get the coroner and Dr. Rodgers to help but neither was available. So, she did it. By phone, Cecil instructed her what to do, step-by-step. Maybe it wasn't against the law after all, since Cecil was instructing her. How many mortician's wives would have done that? The young couple never even knew anything was awry at Hunt & Larkin. Betty received the body, prepared it, and then helped the young couple select a child's casket. She even drove the hearse. I don't think they ever paid for any of it, but then that's how she and Cecil did business. You don't find too many businesses, in any field, doing things like that. It has been a special place," Heddy ended her recollection.

Martha retrieved some quilts kept on hand for family members who might go into shock during their mourning. Each of the four removed her shoes and wrapped up in a quilt. June laid her head on one arm on the couch, Martha Rae on the other end. Louise placed the chair cushions on the floor to form a mattress, and Heddy pulled a mattress from a casket in the selection room. Like antique, spinning tops who had lost their momentum, the four fell asleep, breathing the sweet carnation-filled air.

Outside, just beyond the rippled Palladian window, on the freezing stone sidewalk, lay hundreds of thousands of damp, dead leaves, turned almost black by the winter night. The tail of a northern wind blew around a dozen vacant buildings holding the empty parking lot hostage. The long line of bare maple trees seemed to vanish in the cold, black sky. The only warmth outside the funeral home, was a suspended yellow blinking light at the corner, keeping a lost sparrow intermittently warm and awake.

CHAPTER NINE

E arly the next morning, the phone rang. Louise, asleep on the floor near the desk, sat up and answered the annoying ringing. It was the coroner calling to say he had determined the official cause of death to be heart attack. He wanted to know how to dispose of Betty's body.

"Should I have a funeral home over in Gainesville come and pick her up? Or, do you want Heddy to do it?" Louise told him they would call back by noon. The ringing had also awakened the other sleeping Club members. Instinctively, Martha Rae rose and went to the kitchen. Soon, she returned with the tray and served coffee. Louise then posed the question,

"Girls, what are we going to do? She has to be prepared."

No one said a thing.

"Ok, we ask him to send Betty over here or, we'll have to call a funeral home from somewhere, maybe Gainesville, to come and pick her up. We have to decide," Louise was pushing for a resolution to the question.

Heddy just sat there. Big tears welled up in her eyes for the first time in decades, maybe the first time ever. Embarrassed, she wiped them hoping the others had not noticed. She mumbled,

"You know, I always thought that...that, I could...do...just about anyone. Just about anyone. But, I don't know. I really...don't know."

"I don't know either," June offered supportingly. Martha Rae remained silent.

"Well, we need to make a decision this morning," Louise continued.

Shortly before ten, someone knocked. Martha answered. Of all the wrong times. It was an express mail agent, with an overnight delivery. Martha signed for the packet. Louise opened the blue and white envelope which bore the return address, "Loemann & Loemann." Of course, the firm had not known of Betty's death. Even if they had, it probably would not have made a difference. Business was business. Even though Louise had, from the first, been interested in convincing Betty to sell, this now seemed like such an intrusion. She pulled a sealed envelope out of the packet and laid it on the desk without opening it.

Again, the phone rang. It was the coroner. He was

offering to bring Betty to the funeral home and then suggested he might prepare her himself. Without consulting the others, Louise agreed.

Betty Larkin came back to Hunt & Larkin for the last time that morning. The ladies could hear the coroner trying to open the back door of the prep room. He began banging and kicking the door. Heddy chuckled. He must have finally succeeded, because the noise was now just behind the swinging door. No one moved or made a sound.

The door opened slightly and Martha gave a start. The coroner stood half way through the swinging door.

"I...uh...got her in. I have moved her to the table. I really am sorry. I know this is very, very difficult for all of you. She was a wonderful person. Look, I am going to run home and change clothes. I'll be back shortly."

He released the door gently, and it swung back and forth, squeaking with each swing. Heddy's voice was soft.

"I really feel bad about this. I feel like I am letting all of us down, especially Betty."

For the first time in anyone's memory, including that of the Club's oldest member, Louise, Heddy began to weep aloud. These were no longer quiet tears, but a strong and powerful cry, full of emotion and volume. The three other Club members rushed to Heddy whose wail grew louder. Hers was a long, pitiful, honest statement of her frustrations. They held her tightly.

Heddy's tears were obviously more than just sorrow for the loss of her friend. The tears went beyond her guilt of not wanting to embalm this person who had given her friendship and life-long employment despite her frequent abrasive personality. This rush of emotion was an unleashing of almost sixty years of hidden fear and anxiety, of not just one, but three failed marriages, of not completing high school. It was the emotion she had secretly wanted to express when the Davis boy was prepared, but avoided in her usual stoic way. But now, it was ok, not to be a brute. It was acceptable to let everything out here, among the other Club members. Betty's death allowed her that opportunity. Perhaps Betty's passing helped Heddy, more than any of them, to find truth and honesty in discovering those genuine feelings that were kept hidden for so many years. For a quarter of an hour, Heddy openly cried in the arms of her friends.

Suddenly, Heddy sat up from her hunched position on the floor, in front of the couch. The others released her and she pulled her shirt sleeve across her nose and mouth. She cleared her eyes with the palms of her hands. Still overwrought, she spoke,

"You know, Betty didn't even like the coroner. She would be very unhappy with all of us if we let him prepare her. I think...maybe...just maybe, that Betty would want me, or maybe us, to get her ready for her funeral."

Heddy paused to think a second, sniffing her nose, wiping her eyes.

"Never mind, you all probably think it's a..."

"No...no, I don't think it is a bad idea. I think she would be happy that we did it," agreed June.

"Do you mean the two of you do this, or all of us?" Louise wondered, wiping her eyes.

"Anyone who wants to help," Heddy was growing more confident of her mission.

"Yes, but Martha, you wouldn't have to, if you..." June said reassuringly.

"I don't know if I could. I just..."

"We'll take care of her. You answer the phone in case anyone calls," Heddy directed.

The four Club members began standing, relying on each other for support in getting to their feet. Heddy and June started for the swinging door. Louise followed slowly after glancing back again at Martha Rae, who had moved toward the Palladian window.

At the window, Martha Rae placed her face only an inch from the cold glass. She could see the big word across the street on the old hardware store window. Through her own tears and the rippled glass, the word CLOSED appeared larger, more distorted than ever before. As warm air escaped her lungs, fogging the glass, the word vanished.

Martha turned away and walked toward Betty's

desk to wait for calls. She held up the single brown leaf left in the pen holder. She looked at the unopened envelope from Loemann & Loemann. She didn't stop there. Instead, she walked cautiously toward the prep room and placed her left hand flat, softly against the door and gave it a slight nudge. It opened only an inch. Martha Rae stood for a few seconds, peering through the opening, watching her friends. She could see Betty's white hair at the end of the table. The door then opened wide and Martha Rae Allsion went in.

Each woman gave Martha a small reassuring smile. Taking Martha's hand, Heddy led her to her side of the table. She and Martha Rae stood on Betty's right and Louise and June stood on the left. A white sheet was pulled up to the neck and completely covered the lower body. Betty's hair was not too disheveled and she actually looked very peaceful.

"Ok," Heddy began.

"Uh, if y'all don't mind, could we say a short prayer, or maybe, could I say a short one?" Martha asked.

They all agreed, holding hands and *including* Betty.

"Dear Lord, this is our friend. You have already met her. Please take care of her. She is...uh...is..."

"Boo noo noo noos," June said sincerely with a soft Jamaican accent.

"Amen," Martha Rae concluded.

"What we do first is fold back the sheet on the

right side, just below the collar bone. Then we will make a small incision just above that point."

Heddy pulled the sheet back, cut the skin, and then gently clipped a small vein and artery inside the incision.

We are going to attach a small tube to the vein to flush away her blood and then insert the arterial injection tube to embalm."

Heddy turned on the noisy pump equipment, sending fluid into the body until only it alone ran out of the vein tube. She stopped then and closed the incision.

Knowing that Betty would not want her lower jaw to open in the viewing room or at the funeral, Heddy took a small wiring instrument and attached a thin wire to each gum. She gently twisted it to fix the mouth closed.

"In most cases," Heddy informed the group, "a person's lips will stay closed over the teeth, as Betty's do."

Heddy did not have to do anything special to keep Betty's eyelids shut. They did so naturally.

The phone rang. June lifted the received of the black wall phone.

"Hunt & Larkin. Yes. Yes she did. Tuesday morning, yes. Tuesday morning at 10 A.M. It's ok. Things are really...ok. Yes, she was always surrounded by friends, close friends," June looked at the others, "and still is. Yes. Bye."

Next, Heddy used a stainless steel aspirator tube to empty her friend's lower cavity. Her friends found this difficult to watch, so Martha and Louise were sent to Betty's home to get her favorite dress. While they were gone, Heddy closed the small incisions in the abdomen.

Finally, June and Heddy bathed Betty. June shampooed her hair and dried it. By that time, Martha Rae and Louise had returned and all of the friends helped to dress Betty. As Betty's body lay on the table, June arranged her hair in the "Donna Reed" style which Betty loved so much. Years earlier, after finding Mrs. McBride in the chair, Heddy had taught June that the hair of a deceased person is usually fixed as the body reclines on the table.

Martha Rae offered to do Betty's makeup. She was successful in making Betty appear natural.

The whole process took about two hours. When it was finished, the four washed and made their way to the selection room to choose Betty's coffin. The casket supply company had sent a replacement for the damaged white casket with brass handles and the four selected it. They wheeled the coffin to the prep room and carefully positioned Betty in it. They took her to the Blue Room and sat silently.

"I am surprised that it was so easy. I have been afraid of deceased persons ever since my son died. But this was different. I feel very close to Betty," Martha Rae admitted.

"Yes, we did exactly what she would have wanted us to do," Louise thought out loud.

"I didn't think I could do it, but I discovered I could. But only with the help of my three best friends," Heddy confided. Resisting the obvious, June expressed in English, "She was someone special, very special."

As the four visited quietly, a knocking and banging were heard at the back door. The sounds grew louder and then ceased. In seconds, the coroner's voice was heard, from the main parlor.

"Are you here?"

They called for him to come into the viewing room. He apologized for taking so long and then was surprised to find Betty already there. The ladies proudly admitted they had taken care of their friend.

The telephone rang and Martha hurried to answer.

"Hunt & Larkin. Yes. We are very sad about it. Yes. Tuesday, at 10 A.M. at her church. Yes, we all loved her, too."

CHAPTER   TEN

It was a funeral of which Betty would have been proud. The service centered around music and friends. Even the children from the Winnsboro Elementary were included. The service began when June came down to the altar and asked the overflow crowd to stand. They did, and Clarence Little, a black bass singer from Harmony Grove Baptist Church, who was anything but little, stood in the balcony and sang, "I'll Take the Wings of the Morning," a cappella. His resonant voice consoled those gathered, bringing instant tears to every eye.

Once finished, he came downstairs and led the Harmony Grove Baptist Church choir down the aisle behind Betty's casket which was wheeled in by Martha Rae and Heddy. As the choir members proceeded, they sang another spiritual, "You May Have

All Dis World, But Give Me Jesus." The sixteen-member black choir formed a semi-circle around Betty for the last verse and then took seats in the choir loft to the left of the altar.

In her quite way, Betty had done a great deal to improve race relations in Winnsboro. Betty's co-workers felt including the choir was most appropriate. After all, for many years Betty and Cecil had helped the owners of the nearest black funeral home, just across the state line in South Carolina. While blacks and whites didn't normally worship together or bury their dead in the same cemeteries in Northeast Georgia, they did often enjoy each others' singing, particularly at special events. Betty was color blind when it came to skin.

The Rev. Williams then led the congregation in prayer. Following the prayer, Heddy, of all people, read scripture from the New Testament. She chose the passage about the body having many parts. She had apparently read the verse frequently or had studied diligently the previous day or two. Her diction was perfect and all signs of the rough talking Heddy were absent. She reached the verse about the parts of the body speaking to each other:

"The eye can never say to the hand, 'I don't need you.' The head can never say to the feet, 'I don't need you.'"

Heddy paused and then began delivery of the most incredibly touching eulogy one could imagine.

She spoke about her unmotivated and unsuccessful high school days and her failed marriages. She related how Cecil and Betty took her in and helped her develop a sense of pride, self confidence, but most importantly, self respect. Everyone knew that Betty was instrumental in helping Heddy achieve her full potential, and success, as a mortician.

It was Martha Rae's turn. Sitting on the front row, she stood up and led a group of children to the area just in front of the altar. There, she directed the twenty-four elementary children in, "Jesus Loves Me." The purity of the children's voices, mixed with the overwhelming sadness of the occasion, was more than most people could handle. As the singing ended, one of the children stepped to the microphone and delivered an impromptu tribute. She said, "Good-bye Miss Betty. We love you." The little girl took three steps down from the altar area, her long straight blonde hair wafting slightly as she went.

Martha Rae said a few words about Betty's commitment to children in the community and her voice broke as she related how Betty had always wanted a child. Martha sat down and Clarence Little took his position in front of the altar, delivering a prose reading, "Fly Down."

The short poem was often used at local black funerals, but this was a first for a white person's service in this community. According to some, the reading came from a book of poems printed at the turn of the century. Clarence had read the piece so often during his life he needed neither book or notes. The towering man with a rich voice began softly:

Fly down, fly down,
You mighty horse,
Fly down from your perch above;
Come spread your angel wings,
Descend on us like a dove.

Fly down, fly down,
You sleek black stallion,
To carry your faithful back home;
Pick up our sister here,
No more shall she roam.

Mount her on your sturdy back,
And fly across the sky,
Take this humble servant, Lord
Never, never to die.

All her many years,
In good times and bad,
She kept her faith, oh God;
Making others glad.

Fly down, fly down,
And pick her up,
Take her to your side, oh Lord,

And share with her your eternal cup;
Spare her from Death's sword.

Despite our fear,
And loss so great,
Oh God, we pray to you;
Take our friend,
Make her whole;
And give her life anew.

It is now time,
To bid farewell,
To let her go above;
Fly down, fly down,
Take her home,
We thank you for her love.

Higher, higher,
The pegasus flies,
Our lamb astride her ride;
Taking her to precious Jesus,
For ever and ever by his side.

She disappears, we can not see,
Long gone from our sight,
She lives with you now, oh God;
We kiss her a final,
Good night.

Not a sound was made in the sanctuary as Clarence finished the reading. No cries, no movement. He simply walked over to the choir loft and took a seat. Just as Betty had always made everything seem all right, now Clarence, speaking of Betty had had the same effect at the funeral.

Louise came forward to the microphone and related what Winnsboro might had been like had Betty and Cecil not come to the town after the War. She felt that Betty was like her sister. She told that she and Betty frequently argued over spending habits and that Betty almost always won. Louise told the crowd about Muzaun Briggs and how the Larkins always wanted the best for those in the community. Only once, did Louise have to adjust her glasses to allow for her tears. She told the congregation that she felt guilty about the recent events concerning the attempted Hunt & Larkin buyout. She ended by saying she had always wanted the best for Betty and that now she had it.

June came up to the pulpit and sang a Jamaican song about love which was often sung at funerals on the island. Rev. Williams again stood, gave the benediction and invited everyone to attend the graveside service. Heddy and June wheeled the casket back down the aisle and the mourners followed.

The coffin was loaded into the shiny hearse and the funeral procession, led by a Winnsboro police officer, went down Main Street as the winter sun shone brightly through the bare branches overhead. The officer turned right, at the end of Main, and drove toward the cemetery, just beyond the new loop.

Heddy's strong hands held tightly to the steering wheel of the big hearse. Her eyes, which had been focused on the rear lights of the police motorcycle just in front, took a quick look out the left window at the string of Mega Mart type stores. People were busy going into and out of the giant discount businesses. Some of those waiting to leave the parking lot, at the new traffic light which had been green in their direction, probably did not know Betty and were annoyed at having to wait for the long train of cars to pass. Heddy looked into the rearview mirror to see the spray of flowers on Betty's casket and for the second time in three days, her eyes were wet. Her damp eyes moved back to the motorcycle in front of her. The flashing blue light was a blur.

At the grave site, six wrestling team boys in their letter jackets, serving as pall bearers, unloaded the brass and white coffin. It was placed on the lowering device but remained stationary as Rev. Williams spoke the final prayer and Betty's four closest friends sat in green draped chairs on the front row.

After the crowd of about three hundred dispersed, Heddy, Louise, Martha Rae and June returned to their seats under the forest green tent and sat quietly in the front row of chairs. The four ladies gently held each others' hands as the afternoon winter sun warmed the forest green tent. Finally, they rose to their feet and Heddy motioned to Mr. Jackson, the grave attendant. Heddy and June drove away in the hearse; Louise and Martha Rae followed in the limo. Once they were out of sight, Mr. Jackson completed the job of placing Betty to rest.

Few had touched this small rural town as Betty had over the years. It would be difficult to find anyone in Winnsboro who had Betty's sensitivity and savvy. She was truly unique. She had lived in Winnsboro for more than fifty years. But she was more than just a resident. She was the very fabric of the community. A fabric that, now, seemed so unraveled.

C H A P T E R   E L E V E N

F ollowing the funeral, hundreds of Betty's friends gathered at Hunt & Larkin for lunch. It was a special time because many had said goodbye to friends and loved ones in the same building. It was even more special because Betty had taken care of most of those families in *their* times of sorrow.

A warm front had blown up from the coast the evening before, and the afternoon winter temperature was in the 70's. The low humidity made the skies over Mount Yonah a pristine blue. Yonah only appeared this clear in the winter. During the spring and summer, an abundance of moisture in the air almost always shrouded the peak in a light blue haze.

There were so many people to share the meal at the picnic, that John Criswell, Mr. Morgan's replacement as the Sunday school teacher, organized several teenagers to bring tables over from the fellowship halls of both the Baptist and Methodist Church. The tables were set-up around Hunt & Larkin. The afternoon sun, streaking through the bare maple branches, provided unusual patterns and shadows on the laughing faces. Several hundred people in the community celebrated Betty's loving kindness.

Some teenage boys were throwing a football beside the hundred-year-old building and one wayward pass nearly went through the giant Palladian window. Parents chased the group across the street to an open area beside one of the churches. The window was safe.

The low angle of the winter sun exaggerated the texture of the aging paint on the ship-lap siding of Hunt & Larkin. The paint on the wood siding was crackled from a multitude of coatings. For the most part, layer upon layer of paint provided the wood a protective covering, but the surface was fractured with tiny pits and crevices only noticeable upon very close scrutiny. Some areas near the foundation were rotted. From a distance all seemed smooth and unaged, stronger than ever. Most of those gathered for the occasion had never looked close enough to see the truth. To them, Hunt & Larkin had always been there, always would be.

As the sun's rays drifted closer to the top of Mount Yonah, the shadows of the bare maple trees moved from the picnic tables to the exterior walls of the grand white building. The network of shadowy lines looked like arthritic, knobby fingers. The lower shadows looked like giant bony wrists, and against the upper gables stretched long, thin fingertips, gently folding over the roof, as if a skeleton were holding the house securely in place.

At one point, the shadow of a maple was projected through the giant window and on the floor and wall inside. The pattern of branches, mixed with the pattern of wood window framing, caressed the couch, chairs, and century-old hardwood flooring. A few thin fingery lines traveled up the swinging door and ended there. The knobby hands quickly faded, as did the guests, and evening arrived.

Louise, Martha Rae, June, and Heddy went in. It was December 9th. The four ladies sat in the main room. Surprisingly, Louise reminded the Club they had some business to think about.

"With Betty gone, in the next few days we will need to decide what to do with the offer by Loemann & Loemann."

"What to do with the offer?" Martha Rae asked.

"That's not really any of our business, is it?" Heddy questioned.

"Won't the funeral home be sold and the funds placed in Betty's estate?" June wondered aloud.

"Not exactly." Louise got up and went to Betty's desk and began going through drawers. She was searching for something. Then she opened the small mahogany box on top of the desk. In it were the five Christmas envelopes. One to each of them, and one addressed to Betty. Louise confessed.

"Ladies, several weeks ago Betty asked me to do something I urged her not to do. In light of the conflict initiated by Loemann & Loemann's offer, and because she cared greatly for each of us, she requested I have legal papers prepared to give full ownership of Hunt & Larkin . . . to the four of us and herself. Each of us, including Betty's estate, is to own twenty percent of this business. She wanted us to have it, to make up our own minds about the future of Hunt & Larkin.

Louise handed a leaf-covered envelope to each of the ladies, retained the one with her name on it, and placed the one marked "Betty" back in the mahogany box. They sat quietly, opening the carefully-wrapped envelopes. Each read her own legal paper silently.

Still lying beside the wooden box was the unopened Loemann & Loemann envelope, sent several days earlier via express mail. Louise opened the envelope using a brass letter opener in the pen holder. She slid out a notarized letter from Mr. Kline. The offer had been raised to $800,000.00. Louise's mouth dropped. She quietly sat down, figured in her mind each lady's share and announced the most recent news to the others.

"That means, I suppose, that each of you can enjoy $160,000 as soon as arrangements can be made to probate Betty's will and then sell to Loemann & Loemann, or to whomever."

The Club was speechless for some time.

"June, this means you can retire to Jamaica," Martha Rae observed.

"Yes, and Martha Rae, you can move to Texas to be near your family," Heddy added.

"And, Heddy, you can move to Orlando and buy a condo at Disney World!" Martha exclaimed.

They marveled at the possibilities and remained silent again for a while.

Breaking the silence, Louise uncharacteristically suggested,

"Of course, we don't have to sell. It's just an offer to buy."

They all thought about this. Selling would mean giving in to the big business investors who knew no one in the community. As Betty knew so well, it would mean turning off the last business light in downtown Winnsboro. To sell would also give Loemann & Loemann an opportunity to buy downtown and develop its mini-mall. That would be nice, but it would mean virtually no local ownership of any major business or property in the town. The community would be funding the salaries of fat-cat managers and investors who would rarely, if ever, come to Winnsboro. It would also mean having a new funeral home in town after one hundred years. A new building and probably a new staff. It would be a funeral home run by outsiders who knew nothing of these local people or their past. Strangers would perform the last, and most intimate surgical procedures on every deceased Winnsboroite, perhaps including the four women, themselves.

Suddenly, Martha Rae, sorting out her thoughts, spoke.

"I don't think we should sell. Not at all!"

"Me either," June agreed, carefully.

"Maybe we should just keep Hunt & Larkin alive," Heddy adding to the possibility.

"I'll agree to whatever the three of you want," Louise compromised. Her lip twitched, but only very slightly.

"Let's do it! Don't sell! Keep it alive!" They all joined in, becoming more and more excited at the thought. "We'll show Loemann & Loemann who owns Winnsboro," Heddy asserted.

"This is OUR funeral home and they can't have it, ever!" Martha Rae chimed in.

"WE could build a new facility on the property out at the cemetery," Louise proposed.

"Or we could keep the lights on here, downtown, forever!" Heddy yelled.

"We could open our own mini-mall in the vacant buildings and plant flowers this spring all over downtown," June said excitedly, and then added, "We'll have antique shops, art galleries, and maybe re-open the drug store as a small restaurant serving Jamaican specialties!"

"It'll be a great place for tourists to come when they want to forget Atlanta for a few hours, " Louise agreed.

The four women jumped wildly around in a big circle. They hollered, yelled, and danced. It was joyful chaos. They chanted,

"Boo noo noo noos!!! Boo noo noo noos!!!"

C H A P T E R   T W E L V E

I n the months following Betty's funeral, Louise and Tom McBride fought Loemann & Loemann courageously. The community split on the idea of a new mini-mall in the vacant downtown area to be developed by the Atlanta corporation. Many wanted the area revitalized, but others realized that the proposal meant further loss of local ownership of Winnsboro.

Twelve months later, again in December, following a light snow, tension had built to a peak. Half the community wanted all development along the loop to stop. Others, who had moved to Winnsboro in recent years wanted more and more stores built along the by-pass. Talk of new nationally owned fast-food establishments went around town. Each week, the newspaper carried articles until emotions in the community reached a frenzy. Letters to the editor were equally divided on the issue. Heddy, Martha, Louise, and June photocopied the Loemann & Loemann fraud article sent to Martha from her brother in Texas. They paid some local kids to put copies on windshields of cars at the parking lots of Mega-Mart and the new food stores.

Each side organized, and a huge demonstration was planned on the last Saturday of the month. Giant banners were carried by supporters of the "old" Winnsboro, who met in a rally in downtown near the icy maples. In the Mega-Mart parking lot, newcomers assembled and carried signs and placards demanding progressive development of Winnsboro. A rumor started that the two groups were going to march toward each other around noon...which they did.

Television reporters from Atlanta got wind of the rally, from the paper editor, and covered the town like ants. Helicopters buzzed overhead as the two groups headed for a confrontation. Reporters from a national television news magazine show appeared covering the biggest event ever held in Lanier County.

The marchers from downtown chanted,

"Corporate money isn't funny. Take your pay and go away!"

Leading the group from downtown was Heddy, on her Harley, decked out in black leather. She slowly inched along the street, revving the bike frequently to display her esprit de corps. June was riding sidesaddle, while Louise and Martha Rae followed behind on foot, each wrapped snugly in winter coats. Several hundred sign-carrying supporters followed, chanting as they walked.

Mr. Kline, several non-Winnsboro store managers and many hourly workers from the discount stores marched from the other direction. They saw the event as an opportunity to kill off the old downtown support once and for all.

A few minutes after noon, the two groups met in front of Winnsboro Springs Park. The tree-loaded park looked liked a winter wonderland, covered from several days of snow. A dozen state prisoner workers, under close security from armed guards, were in the park changing light bulbs in tall, quaint Victorian light poles, when the two groups clashed on the street running along side the park.

The most aggressive protesters in each group met first and yelled awful things at each other. Soon, the disagreeing people spread into the park, and the anger turned physical. Mr. Grogan's wife, a sixty-year-old quack took her sign and banged it over the head of a rather well dressed young man in a red nylon ski jacket.

John Campos, one of three local policeman, grabbed the older lady and attempted to hold onto her. Unfortunately, it was too late, the crowd of emotional supporters turned into a melee. Two men rolled around on the ground, knocking over a ladder on which one of the prisoners was standing. Half a dozen light bulbs whooshed into the soft white snow, followed by a twelve-inch frosted, round globe which shattered on the head of one of the two bullies. The prisoner hid behind a guard for protection.

Three teenage boys wrestled near the water springs, for which the park was named, until two of them fell into the freezing water. The springs had brick lined bottoms, only two feet below the surface, which made the plunge cold but not life threatening. The kids, dripping wet, ran to the sixty year old community building at the other end of the park, where more fighting had erupted.

The massive rock and timber community house, reached by way of a wide foot bridge, was built by the Works Project Administration in 1932. Members of the Kiwanis were decorating it for their annual Christmas party to be held in the early afternoon. The boys warmed themselves by the oversized rock fireplace, forgetting the dispute that caused both to be soaking wet. The two hung their soggy winter shirts on the massive wood mantle, which ran over a dozen feet in length.

Outside, under giant rough hewn timbers that supported the rock porte cochere, two men took swings at each other, until finally one was knocked into a daze. A group of angry women ran toward the standing roughneck, grabbed him by the arms and legs and deposited him on the brick lined driveway.

Soon, more people ran toward the old community building and fighting erupted inside the structure. White paper table clothes were ripped off the long tables as people scrambled from one aisle to the next. Two, ten-gallon water coolers, filled with sweetened and un-sweetened tea, went flying through the air and crashed on the slick, log walls. Three sets of French doors flew open and the fighting moved out to a rock balcony that overlooked the park and the drained swimming pool. Louise, standing at the edge of the balcony, grabbed an un-sliced roast beef, raised it over her head and zonked her twin, Mr. Kline, who was down below on the ground, hiding. The beefy hind-quarter hit him square on the head, dislodging a toupee, which flew away with the roast.

Mr. Jones, former owner of the hardware store, took a restaurant tray filled with potato salad and tossed the salad over the two story rock balcony onto several female workers from Mega-Mart. A tub of spaghetti was thrown through the air and crashed into one of six wagon wheel chandeliers hanging from the rough hewn ceiling timbers. The Kiwanian ladies watched in horror as Christmas tree decorations and catered food covered every log wall of the community house, a structure that had stood more than six decades as a monument to community spirit and pride.

News cameras and radio reporters captured the whole sordid event. Helicopters buzzed overhead tap-ing the march, the fighting in the park, and the fighting around the old stone building. Everyone in Atlanta and across the state would see the Battle of Winnsboro on the evening news.

The fighting ended when several Lanier County sheriff deputies fired their guns into the air outside the community house, causing the crowd of protesters to disperse. Within minutes, the only people left around the rock structure were the Kiwanians and Mr. Grogan. The latter was trying to talk the local man-in-blue into releasing the loud and angry Mrs. Grogan who the policeman had handcuffed to his own wrist, mainly for her own protection.

People in the community were so embarrassed by what they saw on the Atlanta evening news, and on the network magazine show three weeks later, that the whole issue was ignored for several months. People just refused to talk about it.

In late spring, with encouragement from the four Funeral Club members, the downtown property owners initiated a partnership. They named it Winnsboro Development, Inc. which provided low interest loans for those merchants interested in establishing new businesses downtown. The development group included most of the owners of the vacant buildings, as well as Louise. Tom McBride sent several unfriendly letters to Mr. Kline and, by summer, Loemann & Loemann was no longer interested in Hunt & Larkin. They sent McBride a letter stating they not only had lost interest in the funeral home but had discontinued any idea of building their own facility at the cemetery or any where else in Lanier County for that matter. They also had *THE BANNER* run a story that the mini-mall plans were canceled. The development members had made it clear to the outside business world that the future of Winnsboro, like its resources, were to stay in the community.

Members of Winnsboro Development had architectural plans drawn up for converting the dozen buildings facing the Square into a series of shops, restaurants and boutiques. The old movie theatre was to be renovated and to become a performance space, utilized as a summer-rep program by a near-by college theatre department. Soon, downtown Winnsboro was again alive with economic success. Of course, the Mega-Mart, Save-Mart and regional food stores were still busy every moment their doors were open, but downtown had found a new niche.

The local developers contacted regional artists who were interested in establishing an art gallery. Martha Rae oversaw the planting of thousands of flowers all over downtown. Colorful canvas awnings were fitted over many of the windows and doorways. Downtown Winnsboro had experienced a renaissance. The brick streets took on new life and the old parking lots began to fill once again.

Tom McBride agreed to underwrite the building of a new funeral home at Winnsboro Cemetery, renting the new facility to the four ladies, an idea all of them thought perfect.

The building was finished the following spring and Louise, Martha, Heddy and June began plans to move out of the deteriorating, one-hundred year old Victorian home of Hunt & Larkin. One weekend when there were no clients at the funeral home, the ladies packed up things with help from the high school wrestling team and local church members.

Heddy and June packed away the many instruments, while others helped Martha and Louise place office supplies into boxes. Some men came later in the day and helped load filing cabinets, caskets, and the big leather couch into several U-Haul trucks. The heavy prep table was loaded last.

The exterior facing on the new funeral building at the Winnsboro cemetery was old Chicago brick which gave it a weathered look, even though it was new. The grounds had been meticulously landscaped by the builder and a matching brick fountain on the front lawn sprayed water into the warm summer air, capturing it below in a pool stocked with enormous gold fish. Helpful men moved furniture and caskets into the building through the front door. Heddy, backed the hearse up to the fancy cement ramp that led conveniently to the new, extra-wide metal door of the prep room at the rear of the building.

Heddy and June jumped out, opened the back door of the Cadillac, and pulled out a wheeled stretcher. They loaded several boxes on top and gently led the cart to the door. Heddy reached in her pocket, pulled out a shiny brass key and inserted it in the lock of the new metal door. She turned the key and pulled on the large handle. Nothing moved. She turned the key again, heard the deadbolt release and pulled harder a second time. Nothing budged. Heddy's look pierced June, who just smiled. She grabbed the handle with both hands, placed her right foot on the new brick border around the door, and gave a third jerk.

"Open damnit, you piece of crap!"

The door burst open as Martha gave a gentle shove from the inside. Heddy landed on the gurney as June laughed and Martha observed,

"Almost like home?!"

The paint had barely dried on the new walls before a call to pick up the first client was received. Mrs. Gordon Smith, a widow who had recently moved to Winnsboro, from Atlanta, was on the other end of the line. Louise answered. "Hunt & Larkin. May I help you?"

"I need your help!"

"Yes?"

"Please help. Mr. Jeeber is dead, and I need help."

"Where do you live, ma'am? I'll call an ambulance."

"Twenty-six, Chattahoochee Trail. You don't need to send an ambulance, the old gentleman IS dead."

Heddy told the upset woman she would be right

there. The experienced mortician picked up the phone, dialed the coroner and gave him the address. She and June jumped in the hearse and headed for Chattahoochee Trail, about two miles away. They pulled up to the home and saw an older woman sitting on the front porch steps. Heddy and June approached the elderly woman gingerly, and spoke softly.

"Ma'am, did you call? We're from Hunt & Larkin."

"Yes. Yes. It's Mr. Jeeber. He's dead. By the back door. I just don't know..."

June sat down beside the white headed lady and lovingly put her arm around the woman's bony shoulders which were covered by a cotton dress. Heddy went around the house to the back yard. Her firm hand grasped the black metal latch on the wooden gate, swinging it open. The smell of freshly cut grass hung in the summer air. A stalled lawn mower sat near-by, its engine still crackling with heat.

The red-haired woman went to the porch but saw nothing. She looked on the right side and then the left. No body. Nothing. Heddy started back around and then saw a large lump, just inside the screen door. She stepped up to the door and slowly eased the screen door open. Motionless, there lay Mr. Jeeber...a cat. A dead cat. And not just any old dead cat, but a giant dead tabby cat.

Heddy moved her hand to the top of her head and

scratched the red mop. Chuckling, the sweet giant went back to the front of the house to see June holding the woman securely. Heddy smirked.

"Oh, June, Mr. Jeeber is by the back screen door. Why don't you take a look?" June soon returned, obviously holding back a giant, Boo noo noo noos. June gave Heddy a little smile and sat again by Mrs. Smith, asking her how it happened. The lady said he must have died of old age. June told the widow they would take care of Mr. Jeeber. Heddy's eyes opened widely. The black Jamaican went to the hearse, opened the back door and pulled out a folded black bag. The two morticians went around back, both stifling laughter. June stuffed the enormous striped cat into the bag, explaining,

"Black bag, my favorite!" They smiled.

Once more, the two women consoled Mrs. Smith and then loaded the bag into the back of the hearse, stopping briefly at the cemetery to bury the "gentleman." Personal attention was always the first concern of these caring ladies who possessed strong spirits.

A few weeks later, Louise, Heddy, Martha Rae, and June leased, to a local family, the old vacant funeral home. It became a restaurant, The Maple Leaf. Within just twelve months, many of the ideas of the little Club had become reality.

Hunt & Larkin had balanced precariously on the edge of survival the last few months of Betty's life. She would have been proud of her Club members had she lived and been a part of the re-development of down-town. The four women, with the help of a few other positive thinkers, turned a nightmare into a living dream.

By the following spring, almost every building had been remodeled and leased. Jones' Hardware was an art gallery for local artists and the owners had scheduled their first show by a regional water color artist. The space originally owned by M. F. Moses became a pottery boutique with craftsmen working in the back. Copeland's Drug Store was remodeled as a "turn of the century" ice cream and candy parlor. A recent college photography graduate, and former Winnsboro High graduate, set up shop in a space that was, ironically enough, a photographer's studio thirty years earlier. A book store was also added.

A downtown dedication was held on the steps of the new Maple Leaf Restaurante. White wrought iron tables with green and white striped umbrellas lined the sidewalk under the maple trees. After the dedica-tion, lunch was served inside, and outside, the new restaurant, formerly the Hunt & Larkin funeral home. Louise, Heddy, Martha Rae and June sat inside, at a table directly in front of the giant Palladian window they knew so well.

"Well, this is one thing I never imagined we would be doing in this room," Heddy observed.

They all agreed.

"They have really turned our old building into a

showplace. It makes you wonder why it didn't happen sooner," Martha Rae continued.

"Yes, having the kitchen behind the swinging door gives new meaning to the words, Preparation Room!" June had caused her friends to laugh.

"Do you think Betty is watching us?" Louise asked.

The sound of other excited restaurant chatter consumed the silence as the four thought.

"No doubt," Heddy reflected, speaking for them all.

"I wish she were here to enjoy this black bean soup with crab meat, don't y'all?" June asked.

They all nodded assent.

"You know, I don't think you even have to learn over to the vase to catch the smell of this fresh, blue carnation," Martha chuckled.

Again, agreement was signaled by quiet laughter.

"We really did it. Betty wanted us to make the decision about Hunt & Larkin. She wanted us to decide about keeping our jobs, or selling out. We kept our jobs. We kept downtown Winnsboro," Heddy explained.

"And we kept Hunt & Larkin, we just gave her a new face. Don't y'all think the community really enjoys having the new building at the cemetery? It's really convenient for mourners," Louise observed.

The ladies again agreed.

Soon, baked grouper with special Jamaican seasonings was delivered to the table and the four enjoyed themselves.   June had shared her famous recipes with the restaurant owners. Finally, the ticket was left, and Louise's aging hand picked it up, surprising the other three ladies. Her lips, sporting lipstick, a birthday gift from June, never noticeably puckered. The Club left a generous tip for the attractive teenage waitress.

The quartet went out the door and down the steps, trying to remember in which direction Louise had parked her car. It was parked away from downtown, to the right, at the end of about eight cars parked alongside the maple trees, which were a brilliant green on this early, summer afternoon. There wasn't room to park on the Square.

Martha Rae, the last Club member out and momentarily confused, turned left down the side walk and glanced across the street to see several ladies entering the former hardware store, to look at watercolor paintings. She didn't recognize the women as being from Winnsboro. The license plate tags on the car, from which they had just emerged, read "Florida."

"Martha Rae?" Heddy yelled up the sidewalk from the parked car, "You are going the wrong way!"

Before turning around, Martha caught a glimpse of a local artist adjusting a clever, handmade wooden sign in the sparkling art gallery window, the same window that once said, "Closed!" Now the sign read,

"OPEN, Please Come In." The word open seemed to stretch clear across the Square.

Martha Rae made a u-turn and her purse accidentally bumped another unknown person eating under the shade of one of the pretty umbrellas.

"Excuse me," she said, and then walked toward Heddy, June, and Louise who were getting in the car. Wanting to yell back, but deciding not to make a scene, she muttered to herself, "No, I think it's the right way."

As Martha Rae approached the car, Heddy coaxed her into the Buick.

"Old lady get your fat fanny in here!"

"I'll be happy to, if you'll slide yours over a bit further." All were amused by the kinder lady's boldness. Heddy moved, Martha slid in and shut the door, part of her blue summer dress hanging out the now locked door. Heddy rolled down her window and whistled loosely through her teeth, to a lone distinguished man crossing the tree-lined avenue. He flashed a beautiful toothy smile back to a shocked red-headed mortician. Martha and June slid back a little in their seats. With Louise at the wheel, Heddy climbed halfway out the left rear window yelling,

"Hey, what's your name?"

The tall, attractive man was slightly embarrassed and kept walking briskly toward the Maple Leaf Restaurante. Heddy yelled again then pulled herself back into the car.

Even without Betty there was a warm feeling, a unity among the girls. Things had changed, as things do. The worn out town had sprung to life. Loemann and Loemann was gone for good. Surprisingly, though, even Louise had changed. She often took on causes the way Betty would have. Her lips seldom twitched.

Once back at the new funeral home, June would grasp Betty's white coffee mug with the bright yellow smiley face and pour herself some Jamaican coffee. Around Martha Rae's neck beside her Texas pendant were Betty's pearls, a gift from the estate that each thought appropriate. Louise would sit at the front desk and place papers in the wooden box that had only kept special things over the years. Heddy would wrestle with the new back door. Even though Betty was gone, somehow she was still part of the little group of women known as the Funeral Club.

CHAPTER TWELVE

ACKNOWLEDGEMENTS

Thanks to the following for making this work a reality:

Leslie, Biggs, Kristal, Daniel, Kirk, Bill,
Rita, Don, Bill, Sara, Sam, Betty, Carlton, Curtis,
Drew, Josh, Brad, Larry, Evie,
and my parents.